THE GIRL IN THE TRIANGLE

Joyana Peters

Amaryllis Press

Dedicated To

My Gramps and Grandma

*Two of my biggest supporters who still continue
to guide me from heaven.*

I thought of you with love today

Your memory is my keepsake

With which I'll never part.

You may be gone,

But you will always be in my heart.

Love One Another

~ Frank Vollmer

Ruth

New York City

Monday March 15th, 1909

740 Days Until the Fire

America, her new home. Ruth shifted her suitcase to her other hand and surveyed the city before her. They'd made it. A lump rose in her throat, and she choked back a sudden instinct to cry. All the hardships they'd faced—the years struggling to survive, escaping from Russia, two weeks traveling in an overcrowded ship, followed by the invasive examinations and interrogations at Ellis Island—all of it was for this. A fresh start in this land of promise. Everywhere she looked there was something new to see. Where there had been a few motor-cars on the roads in St. Petersburg, here they drove by like a perpetual parade. Crisp, linear buildings erupted from the earth and towered higher than she imagined possible, their spires and peaks looking as if they pierced the sky. Shopkeepers in pristine aprons and cuffed shirtsleeves swept the stoops of their freshly scrubbed storefronts.

Ruth sensed palpable energy in the air. People in strange, unfamiliar clothing bustled about, each moving with purpose. She jumped out of the way as a clanging bell rang behind her and a huge metal vehicle drove by her on two parallel rails.

How would she ever adapt to this overwhelming, magical place? She took a deep breath and focused on familiar elements. Sellers pushing carts in the road, hawking their wares. The stream of horses and carriages sharing the street. The smell of animal droppings, body odor and roasting meat. Some things, at least, remained the same.

Ruth turned to her younger sister. "What do you think, Little Bird?"

"It'll do," Ester said.

"It'll do?" Ruth asked incredulously. She elbowed Ester in the ribs and snorted. Ester giggled.

"Girls!" Tatty called. "Don't fall too far behind!"

They scurried to catch up with their parents as they turned onto a new block. Ruth couldn't imagine getting lost in this city her first day. She didn't even know the address of their new home.

Ruth froze in awe as they turned the corner. Tatty gestured at the overflowing pushcarts of food and *tchotchkes*. "See? I told you the marketplace was a slice of home. It's prime real estate, Orchard Street."

A slice of home? There was more here than home had ever offered! There were pushcarts lined up as far as the eye could see. Piles of fruit towered precariously on more than one cart. There were huge barrels of pickles and fresh loaves of bread; Ruth's stomach growled just looking at the offerings.

Momme squeaked in excitement and squeezed Tatty's arm. "Ooh, look at all that fresh produce, and is that a kosher butcher? It's like the old *shtetl* market back home."

Tatty puffed up like a peacock. "The largest marketplace for kosher goods in New York City, steps from our door. Anything you want, you've got here."

Momme smiled and put her hand on his arm.

Ruth couldn't wait to peruse the marketplace. It was too good to be true. Food they could eat! They'd been promised kosher food on the ship when they bought their tickets. But luckily they'd been warned by a clerk at the office not to actually expect it. The meal offerings for the entire journey were things they could not eat. They had subsisted on nothing but the stale, flat loaves of bread and kosher dried meat they'd packed. They'd even ended up sharing their provisions with other passengers who hadn't gotten the warning.

Tatty was moving again, so Ruth rushed to follow as he led them up a set of steps to a soot-stained brick building. He opened the door with a flourish, gesturing for them to enter. Ruth linked fingers with Ester, and they stepped inside.

They entered a narrow entryway leading to a steep wooden staircase. Despite the bright day, it was dark and musty indoors. The only sources of light were from the front door and people's open apartment doors. Adults congregated in the cramped hallway, chatting while their children played underfoot. They waved and patted Tatty on the arm as he squeezed his family by. Ruth sniffed at the strong smell of cabbage mixed with other cooking aromas.

Tatty took the stairs two at a time and continued to exclaim over how lucky they were to be living here. Ruth stopped listening as she concentrated on navigating the rickety stairs. The wooden banister was shaky and there was only one flickering gas lamp on each landing. They reached the third floor, where Tatty gestured to the first door on the right.

"Here it is, home sweet home." He opened the door and waved them in.

It was tiny. Their house in St. Petersburg was not big or luxurious by any means, but it had been at least triple the size of this place. Here the front door led directly into the kitchen, which consisted of a small prep area next to a stove and a table that took up most of the available space. Tatty excitedly showed them the sink with running water. "See, you turn the faucet and it runs! We never had that back in Russia!"

Momme and Ester oohed and aahed, but Ruth hung back, taking in the rest of the three-room apartment. The last bit of kitchen square footage was occupied by a cot squeezed into the corner next to the stove. Someone was to sleep in the kitchen? Was that Abraham's bed?

The wall between the kitchen and parlor had a huge cutout to let in light from the parlor window, the sole window in the apartment. The only room with a door was the bedroom off to her left, but even that had a cutout in the wall to get light from the main hallway. Strangers could literally look into her parents' bedroom. Ruth felt her heart begin to pound. What happened to those beautiful towering buildings? Where was the privacy and space she'd imagined? Was running water really to make up for living on top of each other?

Tatty came up behind her and put his hand on her shoulder. "Abraham and I got a couch for you and Ester to share in the parlor. It was a *fermisht* to get up the stairs, but we did it!"

Ruth mustered a grateful smile. Tatty led her the two steps to the parlor and left her to unpack. He'd built a little shelf in the corner and tacked a curtain to the top, so she and Ester could store their belongings in the family space. The shelf was crooked and leaned to one side. Ruth shook her head as everything she put on the shelf slid to the right. Tatty had never been much of a carpenter, but it was sweet of him to try.

She tucked her now empty suitcase behind the couch, already missing the private bedroom she and Ester had shared back in Russia. To imagine, missing something as silly as a door! She sighed and opened the parlor window to look down below. The sidewalk was thick with people, the air crowded with the barks of street vendors whose strangely-accented Yiddish was at once familiar and strange. Inside the apartment, her family's laughter and raised voices could be heard from the too-near kitchen. She closed her eyes and tried to block it all out. The sacrifice of peace, quiet and privacy would be worth it for the opportunities America could offer. She was sure of it.

"What are you looking at, Ruth?"

Ruth turned to see Ester standing in the doorway. "Just taking a moment. Everything's so overwhelming."

"Ya, I can't believe we're really in America," Ester said. "Momme's wasting no time. She's already reorganizing, claiming men have no idea how to set up a kitchen. And interesting news, Tatty says I have to attend school."

"Attend school? But you haven't gone in years."

"Tatty says they have laws here about it. Can you imagine?" Ester shook her head in disbelief. "I'm not sure I'll know where to begin." She sat down on the couch with a thud.

"Are we really going to share this couch or are you going to make me sleep on the floor?"

Ruth smirked. "Depends where you put your smelly feet. One slip near my face and you're on the floor. And you'll be a natural at school again."

"It'll be nice to learn again," Ester said with a

shrug. "The prospect seems kind of terrifying though. Learning English, starting over in a new country. But Tatty is so excited for us to take advantage of America's opportunities. He says there are night classes for you."

Ruth chewed her lip. The idea of sitting in a classroom with people staring at her sounded far from enticing. She was far too old and out of practice. They'd think she was an idiot.

"We'll see. I might be too busy." She fiddled with the ragged edge of the curtain. "We'll have much to do, setting up the house and getting money coming in."

Ruth wasn't surprised her father was focused on exploring education opportunities. Back home in Russia he'd been a *hakham*, spending his days debating the *Talmud* with other scholars and rabbis. He valued education above all else, and believed understanding the written word encouraged rightful actions. He even encouraged Ruth and Ester to read and discuss topics from the *Torah* to better understand their moral purpose in life. One of her favorite memories of their life in Russia was sitting in front of the fire, debating her father and brother.

Ruth felt the devastating pang of loss when she thought of Jeremiah, even now—four years and two months after his death. She imagined the grief crushed her father, too. He'd had big plans for Jeremiah, who was to attend university and join Tatty in his studies. Instead, Tatty lost both Jeremiah and his own status in one day, and was forced to escape to a new life in America as a peddler.

"There's a lump," Ester complained, testing to see if she'd fit stretched out on the couch.

Ruth crossed the room to sit next to her sister. She scowled as she felt the bulge herself.

"Your side!" they yelled at the same time.

"Fine, we'll draw straws," Ester said. "Or you could just take it because you're nicer?"

Ruth put her hands on her hips. "I'm also older."

"Just by three years." Ester pouted.

"Ah, and yet those three years make all the difference," Ruth said with a wink.

Ester stuck out her tongue at Ruth and jumped up, crossing the room to her own small bag of belongings to unpack. Looking back over her shoulder, she asked, "So, are you nervous about seeing Abraham? Did you see his cot in the kitchen? You're practically sleeping next to each other."

Ruth's heart quickened at the mention of his name. Abraham. The man she'd worshipped since childhood but hadn't seen in four years. She looked away from Ester's expectant gaze. She had seen the cot, but hadn't processed the full impact of it. Ester was right. It was less than five feet away. And with that awful cutout in the wall, he'd be able to see right in. Where would she change?

She swallowed hard as her stomach swirled. "I hadn't really thought about the sleeping arrangements. I've just been focused on seeing him again."

Ester grinned. "You must be so excited. Your engagement can finally be official!"

"It will be a welcome change from sharing letters." Ruth ran her hand through her hair. "But I'm also a little nervous. I mean, he's a man now. What if he no longer enjoys my company?"

"What *narrishkeit!* That's ridiculous,*"* Ester said and swatted her hand as if Ruth's words were a fly. "If anything, he'll find you even more interesting now."

They were interrupted by the sound of a key turning in the lock.

"Guess it's time to find out," Ester said with a grin. "*Mazel tov.*"

Abraham

Abraham wiped his brow as the factory's closing bell rang. Finally. He scanned his cutting station to ensure his order was complete. He could not be held back today. Today he was seeing the girl he was to marry for the first time in four years.

He cupped the stacks of measured sleeves and shirtwaist fronts and backs between his hands so they stood uniformly tall. Scooping up a few straggling scraps, he tossed them in the basket underneath the table. Satisfied, he turned away to stretch. After hunching over for the past ten hours, his back protested against straightening to his full six feet.

He grimaced in pain as Yankel clapped a hand on his back.

"Ready?" his friend asked, grinning. He elbowed Abraham in the ribs. "Don't want to keep your lady waiting. I hope you made your bed this morning so she doesn't think you're a slob."

"Lay off, won't you? You're like a buzzing mosquito," Abraham grumbled. He fumbled for his cap in his pocket and got in line for the stairs. The guard was taking longer than usual pawing through bags. The owners must have clamped down again.

"Touchy. The nerves must be setting in." Yankel laughed and followed. "Hm, I wonder if she'll swoon seeing your ugly mug again, or run the other way?"

Abraham shot him a dirty look and nodded to the guard before pushing through the exit door to the stairwell. He took off down the stairs, weaving his way through the chatting workers.

Yankel called after him and caught up, grabbing Abraham's arm. "Abe, I'm just gassing you."

Abraham stopped on the stair and exhaled, clutching the railing. The workers behind protested and pushed past, anxious to escape outside.

Yankel joined him on the step and pushed him gently to move again. "Look, no fooling now. You're nervous. I get it."

Abraham gave a short nod. They finished their descent and pulled their caps on as they stepped out to the street. They stood blinking against the bright sunlight, their eyes adjusting after the pitch black of the stairwell. Action swirled around them in the busy street. Workers talked over each other, making plans for their one free night of the week. Shopkeepers brought trash to the curb and scrubbed windows as they prepared to close for the night. Behind them the Asch building threw its imposing shadow—the apex of it all, literally dividing the city block at its door step.

The two men stood in silence a moment. Abraham finally turned to Yankel. "Am I a nut?"

Yankel pulled back in surprise. "Of course not."

"Even if I'm alone in holding on to the Old World?"

Yankel tilted his head and began walking before he answered. "You're not alone in holding on to tradition. You have a unique connection we can't all share. You're blessed in that."

Abraham pondered his friend's response. "So,

you'd participate in an arranged marriage?"

"Turning the tables, eh?" Yankel rubbed the back of his neck. "I don't know. I've lived without family meddling for so long."

"What about your sister?"

Yankel smiled. "I think we both know my sister says plenty. But Chayele and I both keep out of each other's business for sanity's sake." He stooped to adjust his shoelace. When he straightened again, he asked, "Where is this coming from anyway? You've lived like a celibate priest since I've known you, never once expressing doubts about Ruth."

Abraham shrugged. "I don't know. Too much time with my thoughts I suppose."

Yankel grabbed Abraham by the arm and attempted to look him in the eye, difficult since Yankel was a foot shorter. "Stop building this up. Are you to marry this girl one day? Yes. Is it today?" Yankel shook his head. "No. Focus on your reunion. You've always spoken about how much you enjoyed her company in the past. Enjoy it!"

He looked up at the street sign and saw they had reached Ludlow Street. "And here is where I leave you, my friend. Been dreaming of a pastrami on rye from Iceland and Katz's all day."

Abraham smiled. "Enjoy. And…thanks."

Yankel grinned, offered a jaunty wave, and strode off to the deli.

Abraham watched Yankel disappear into the crowd and pondered his friend's advice. Enjoy it? He wished it were that simple. His blessed connection to the Old World was also his curse. How could his friend understand that everything about his future with Ruth hinged on the sins of his past?

He began walking again, in the direction of the home he'd shared with both his father and Ruth's father since they'd arrived in America.

He thought of Yankel's description of him living as a celibate priest. It was true he'd never pursued the freedom many of his peers enjoyed in America. Saturday nights on the Lower East Side were a world away from the *shtetl* back home in Russia.

He'd been tempted. He'd have to be made of stone not to be. He was in awe of the cavalier way his friends boasted of taking different girls dancing or to the movies. They had no ties to a particular person, no expectations of marriage. But at the same time, he felt intimidated by the forthright way girls expressed themselves here in America. He missed the respect for the rituals of courtship from back home. And there was Ruth. Beautiful, raven haired, doe-eyed Ruth.

He'd known he would marry Ruth since they were children. Their fathers were best friends and business partners. Her brother, Jeremiah, was his best friend.

Jeremiah and he had been inseparable. And Ruth tagged along, always two steps behind. Her presence used to annoy him, especially when it hindered the boys from doing something exciting. But Jeremiah always welcomed Ruth. To him, his younger sister could do no wrong.

When he and Jeremiah turned fifteen, their parents started discussing the betrothal out loud. Their fathers jested about sharing grandchildren. Even Jeremiah joked about them becoming actual brothers. He and Ruth, however, avoided the subject.

Then Ruth's thirteenth birthday came. It seemed like overnight she changed from a gangly tag-along to an actual girl. Jeremiah caught Abraham looking at her one day as she moved about the kitchen, her steps suddenly graceful, her dress sculpting her new hips.

"She's my sister, remember," Jeremiah said, yanking Abraham outside.

Abraham shifted away uncomfortably.

Jeremiah poked him in the chest. "I'm serious. I give my blessing only because it's you. I know I can trust you. So, promise me that's true. Promise me you'll always look after her."

Looking at Jeremiah's serious face, it had dawned on Abraham how real it all was. Ruth was to be his wife one day. Their union wasn't just a joke between families. He would be responsible for her. His best friend was depending on him. He licked his lips nervously. "I promise."

"All right then." Jeremiah laughed and offered Abraham a hand to shake. "Just don't ever let me catch the two of you necking."

Abraham's face grew hot as he imagined kissing Ruth. Maybe this betrothal wouldn't be so awful.

Abraham had grinned and looped an arm around Jeremiah's neck to give his head a knuckle rub as they walked back into the house.

Abraham shook his head at the memory. He'd give anything for Jeremiah to still be alive to give him a hard time again.

He looked up and realized he'd reached Orchard Street. Only a few more feet until home. Truth time. Could he face her? He hadn't had the opportunity since that awful day. Although they'd exchanged friendly letters over the years, he had no true knowledge of Ruth's feelings. Would she grace him with one of her heart-melting smiles? Or did she blame him as he blamed himself for Jeremiah not returning home? He sighed as he forced his leaden feet to take the last few steps to the building, and to all that awaited him inside.

R u t h

Monday March 15th, 1909

740 Days Until the Fire

Ruth froze. This was it. Was he nervous also? She tucked a piece of hair behind her ear and smoothed down her dress. She took a deep breath and stepped into the kitchen.

"Ruth," Abraham smiled and held both hands out to her. "You're all grown up..."

He no longer wore a *kippah* on his head, she noticed. He also wore strange clothes, long brown trousers and a white collared shirt tucked into his pants, with a buttoned-up vest over his shirt. The whole look had a sleekness to it that accentuated his broad shoulders and strong arms. He'd even cut his hair short and shaved his face. She'd always admired his looks growing up, but now a sophisticated, handsome man stood before her.

Her stomach swirled and she clutched the skirt of her traditional sarafan dress with its bright colors, billowy fit and bell sleeves. Would he be bored by an old-fashioned girl from home when he'd clearly become so American?

She crossed the room and cautiously took his offered hands. From over his shoulder she saw her mother and Ester ducking their heads to hide their smiles. When Abraham followed her gaze, they quickly turned away and pretended to busy themselves with putting plates on the freshly washed shelves. He chuckled and turned to Ruth.

"Want to go for a walk?" he whispered.

She nodded and reached for her coat on the coat rack. Stopping her, he took it and formally held it out for her. She blushed and turned, allowing him to slide it on her. She fastened the buttons and turned to find Abraham holding the door open for her. The serious, polite man standing there was certainly a change from the trouble-making boy she'd known before.

Was it just maturity, or had his forced departure from Russia and losing Jeremiah changed him? She knew it had changed her.

"So..." she said as they began their descent down to the street.

"So..." he said. "Four years, ya?"

"Four years," she laughed. "Tell me about your life. I've read your letters, but tell me what you haven't written about."

"What I haven't written about?" he asked. "I kept no secrets."

"Oh, I didn't mean you kept secrets," she said. She felt her cheeks grow hot. "I just meant I want to know about the little things. Where are your favorite places to go? What are your friends like?"

"I see what you mean now." He scratched his head. "This is strange, no? We used to know everything."

She swallowed against the lump growing in her throat. "Well, it's a fresh start."

"I suppose it is . . ."

It dawned on her that this was the first time she'd ever been alone with Abraham. The reason they'd known everything about each other before was because they'd always shared Jeremiah. Her brother had been the glue that held the trio together during their adventures and games. With Abraham leaving before a real courtship could begin, and Jeremiah now gone, they were in uncharted waters.

They'd reached the first floor and stood waiting for a lull in the steady stream of residents coming home for the evening. A feeling of trepidation swept over Ruth. All these people lived in this one building? How was it possible?

Abraham grabbed her hand and tugged her as he leapt into a break in traffic. They pushed through the front door to meet the darkening sky. Standing on the building's front steps, Ruth was struck by the beauty of twinkling lights in the windows of the tall buildings around her. A row of glowing street lamps stood tall, lining the street like perfect sentinel soldiers. The result was an enchanting glow cast across the entire city. She had never seen anything like it.

"Beautiful, huh?" Abraham said with a smile.

She nodded, unable to speak. She felt like she had stepped into some kind of faerie world.

Abraham glanced over and then turned to her.

"Do you want to see the factory where I work?"

She twirled a piece of hair. "The Triangle?"

"Ya, it's a shirtwaist factory."

"Shirtwaists?"

"A style of ladies' clothing. The girls here wear two separate parts instead of full dresses."

"Oh." She looked at the women walking below them on the crowded street. Most wore hats and frilly white blouses tucked into different colored skirts that came down to their ankles.

She pointed to a trio of women. "Are those shirtwaists?"

"They're from our factory," he said. "I can tell from the pattern. Come, I'll show you."

He took off down the front steps with Ruth trailing behind, like old times. But as she caught up and they began walking side by side, they fell into another awkward silence. Ruth fidgeted with the button on her coat sleeve while Abraham stared down at the street. Finally, she cleared her throat.

"Do you ever think of him?"

He stopped mid-stride and looked at her. Two men pushed past, one jostling Abraham's shoulder. The jolt seemed to awaken Abraham from his reverie and he pulled her along to step under an empty storefront awning.

He took a deep breath and looked her in the eye. "Jeremiah was my best friend, Ruth. Of course I think of him. Like when I see something funny I know he would love, I think how I can't wait to share it with him. Then I remember I can't." He stared off a moment before clearing his throat. "I think that's what I miss most. His laugh."

She smiled up at him. "He really did have a great laugh, didn't he? It sounded almost like a donkey hee-hawing." She looked at the crowd streaming past them. "I think I miss just talking to him. He had a way of making any problem feel like it could be solved. Like it was you and him against the world."

Abraham reached for her hand. "He's still with you, Ruth." He hesitated. "You know when our fathers began negotiating our betrothal, Jeremiah and I had a conversation. He was looking out for you. As usual."

Tears clouded Ruth's vision at Abraham's words. She could easily picture Jeremiah confronting Abraham with puffed-up bravado.

Abraham took both her hands in his and squeezed them a little too hard. When she wiggled her fingers, he instantly softened his grip. "He asked if I'd care for you as my own. Which I always have. I mean, even back when we were kids, I was in awe of you. Your strength, your bravery, even your persistence." He let out a small chuckle.

Abraham glanced down at the ground and shifted

his weight from one foot to the other.

"Ruth, there may be things we don't know about each other yet, but I'd count myself blessed to spend the rest of my life discovering them with you." He paused before offering her a small smile. "So, will you let me care for you? Will you do me the honor of making this betrothal official?"

Her heart leapt with joy as he spoke. He still wanted her. Despite all the changes and time apart, he still wanted to marry her.

She exhaled. "Yes," she said. "I'll marry you."

He grinned and picked her up, twirling her around, incurring some sideways looks from passers-by. He ignored them, put her down and reached to cradle her face.

"I've dreamed of this moment for the past four years."

A laugh escaped her. She felt herself melt at his touch. "As have I," she said. "I didn't think you would have developed such a romantic streak, though."

"Only with you, Ruth," he whispered.

He straightened and stroked his hand down her arm to find her hand.

"We have to wait until my family arrives to have the wedding, if you don't mind. We still need to save all our money for their passage."

"I'd rather wait," Ruth said, without thinking.

Abraham raised an eyebrow.

"No, I didn't mean—" She broke off when Abraham laughed.

"I understand." He stroked her hand with his thumb. "It might be for the best. We'll have time to get to know each other again."

She sighed in relief. "Exactly. So many things to discover."

He squeezed her hand and tucked her arm into his.

"Why don't we begin now?"

She smiled. "The Triangle?"

"The Triangle. I'll even show you my other favorite stops along the way," he said with a wink.

"I'd like that."

They stepped out from under the awning, back into the heavy crowd moving along the street. But for the first time since her arrival, Ruth didn't feel overwhelmed. She felt lighter, hopeful even. She looked up at her new fiancé's profile. He was a different, more mature version of the Abraham she'd known in Russia. But he was also still the same boy she'd climbed trees and laughed with. Hopefully, they could somehow reclaim some of that joy with each other again.

Ester

Friday March 19th, 1909

736 Days Until the Fire

"What about this one, Momme?" Ester asked, pulling down a big round bowl from the shelf.

Momme shook her head. "No, that will take too much room on the table. Don't these men have any oval shaped bowls?"

Momme stood on tiptoe to look for herself. She picked up two mismatched soup bowls and surveyed the collection remaining. "It's like they each went and got one without even consulting the other."

Ester giggled. "Or that was their way of keeping kosher. Just get a new bowl each time one was used."

Momme sighed. "They're not even similar colors."

Ester put her hand on Momme's arm. "It'll look fine. We'll find a way to bring it all together."

Momme nodded and turned away to dust off the bowl with a dish rag.

"Remember your blue bowl back home?" Ester asked. "The one with the pretty swirls?"

Momme smiled. "My favorite. Your father got me that for our tenth anniversary."

"You'd always arrange the table so that bowl was at the center."

"The perfect focal point," Momme said. "So, you remember my lessons in table setting?"

Ester opened the drawer to get the tablecloth. "Start at the middle—the heart of the meal—and work your way out."

Momme picked up the edge of the heavy piece of wood Tatty had gotten for a table extender. Ester grabbed it from the other side. Together, they navigated it to the table and made sure it was centered. Momme unfolded the tablecloth and laid it flat. Then they walked around to make sure the edges were even.

"Perfect," Momme said with a smile. She

hummed to herself as she fiddled with the bowls and plates. Ester began preparing dessert.

She had found fresh honey at the market and hidden it away as a surprise to make her father's favorite *taiglach*. As she mixed and rolled the dough, her mind wandered as it always did while baking.

She thought back to the last time she'd prepared a *taiglach*, back when the entire family was still together in Russia. They certainly didn't have the money for honey once the men were gone. They'd made do, still keeping *Shabbat*, but only with the bare essentials and what felt like shadows of their former joy. It became the definition of "keeping" *Shabbat*, something obligatory, a habit almost. It was a sharp contrast to days past, when *Shabbat* was the central part of each week with extravagances and festivities aplenty.

She used to spend Friday with Momme and Ruth, preparing the three meals and readying the house for observance. Ester loved the grinding halt to the busyness of the week, which brought the family together. They'd sit and linger over the evening meal, talking about every topic imaginable. Eventually, they'd move to the parlor, where Jeremiah would play the piano and sing. Tatty would grab one of them and twirl them into a dip followed by a silly waltz.

Her hands paused in their rolling as it hit her: Jeremiah would still be missing tonight. All this time she could almost forget he was truly gone, pretending he'd left with Tatty and the others to America. But now that illusion was shattered.

Momme put a hand on Ester's back, jolting her back to reality. "Don't over-roll or they'll get too soft. We want crisp, remember?"

Ester put down the rolling pin. She pulled off a piece of dough and rolled it between her fingers to make a ball to put on the tray.

Momme smoothed a piece of hair from Ester's face. "Well done, Little Bird. Tatty will be so pleased."

Ester looked up. "Was that the door?"

Momme moved to open it. A flock of women stood at the threshold, holding dishes. A young child peeked around the legs of one of the women.

"Hello," Momme said.

Ester wiped her hands and came to the door.

"I'm Hedy and this is Fanny, Golda and Anna. We've come to welcome you and offer you help with your first *Shabbat* in America."

"Oh, thank you," Momme said, looking at Ester. Tatty had said the neighbors were helpful here. A strong community, he'd called it.

But this was their first actual encounter.

Hedy led the women past Momme and Ester into the tiny kitchen.

"We'll want to fold up that cot. We can't lose that precious space," Hedy said, pointing.

Anna and Fanny moved to Abraham's sleeping area and began folding up the blankets. Golda busied herself organizing the dishes by the cooking area as the child hovered nearby. He reached a grubby hand to the rolled dough on the counter but Golda, quick as lightening, swatted it away.

Hedy turned back to Ester and Momme. "We've been hosting Abraham, Samuel and Jacob among ourselves these past years. You'll see that's a common practice here. Joining tables in the building."

"We're delighted to finally meet you all in person. Jacob's been talking our ears off about you ladies," Golda said over her shoulder.

"Thank you," Ester said. "But, mind me asking— how in this space could you possibly join tables?"

The ladies laughed. "Ah, it's usually metaphorical in practice," Hedy said.

"Although we have set up right in the hallway before for special occasions," Fanny called as she and

Anna struggled to fold up the cot.

"But it's usually sharing recipes, extra servings, ingredients, and dishes. Adopting people with no place to go. Whatever is needed, we make it a communal effort," Hedy explained.

She glanced to Momme's half-set table. "I have some pretty napkins I just stitched up. I somehow doubt the men thought to stock up on enough."

Momme broke out in tears. "Oh, that would be wonderful."

Hedy gathered Momme into a hug. "Come, we'll get them now and you can also see where my apartment is for whenever you need."

The two departed and Ester was left with the rest of the whirlwind crew. Fanny and Anna finished folding and putting the cot upright in the corner. They then eased the table over so it was now centered with extra room on either side.

"Ooh, *taiglach*, my favorite!" Golda placed a hand on Ester's arm. "You'll have to give me your recipe so we can compare."

Golda called for her child and she and the other two ladies left as quickly as they'd come.

Ester surveyed the now empty apartment. The ladies' brief presence had really improved it dramatically. Golda had managed to maximize the prep area by unfolding the ironing board to store the dishes the ladies brought there, while also creating more space for chopping. She'd also brilliantly stored extra knives and utensils on the bricks jutting out from the wall behind the stove.

The front door opened and Ruth came in with a marketing basket.

"What happened here?"

She untied her kerchief and looked to put her basket somewhere.

"Our building has a *Shabbat* Crew," Ester said, taking the basket from Ruth. She put it on the ironing board. "Doesn't it look so much better? Almost homey, right?"

Ruth shrugged. "I guess, but we have even less room to move now that the table extension is in."

Ester turned away and rolled her eyes. She returned to the baking trays to finish her rolling.

The door opened and Momme entered carrying a handful of embroidered napkins.

"Good, you're back." She left the napkins on the table and moved over to the basket to rifle through Ruth's purchases.

Ruth hung her coat on the rack. "I got everything

you asked for. Except the butcher said I had just missed the soup bones."

Momme slammed her fist on the ironing board. "The *fershtinkiner!* He said that yesterday and told me to send you back exactly when I did today."

Ruth chewed her lip. "I think he has them pre-sold and just tells you that to keep us coming back."

Momme sighed. "I guess it'll take time to establish ourselves as regular customers. How did the men survive for so long without laying any of this groundwork?"

Ruth laughed. "Really? You honestly picture Tatty knowing what to do with a soup bone?"

Ester snorted from her work over the baking trays, and even Momme chuckled.

"I suppose you're right," Momme said as she pulled out a chair to sit. "So, anything else noteworthy?"

Ruth took out a knife and reached into the basket to start peeling potatoes. "I'm thinking about getting a job. I could work at the Triangle with Abraham."

Ester paused from putting the tray in the oven. "But you'd have to work Saturdays."

Momme looked down into her lap. "I was going to begin taking in sewing here at home. So Tatty could spend more time at synagogue and on his studies again. You could help me with that."

Ruth shook her head. "No, it makes more sense this way. Abraham says we need to save for his family's passage. I have factory experience. Why shouldn't I earn as much as I can to contribute?" She shrugged. "Besides, Abraham is already working Saturdays. What's the difference if I do too?"

Momme leaned on the table to get up. "Let's wait and see what Abraham has to say when he gets home."

The key turned in the lock a moment later.

"I guess we won't be waiting long," Momme said.

Abraham came in, stomping his feet and blowing on his hands.

A b r a h a m

Friday March 19th, 1909

736 Days Until the Fire

Warmth. He couldn't remember the last time he'd come home to a warm apartment. He breathed in the heavenly smells of dinner.

Ruth ran to greet him and his heart jumped in his chest. For the first time, the apartment felt like home.

"Hope you're hungry. Dinner should be ready soon."

Abraham smiled. "Ah, you wonderful *berryers.* My mouth is already watering."

Ruth lay a hand on his arm. "Can we talk?"

"Sure, let me just hang my coat."

He hung his hat and coat and reached for her hand.

"Something wrong, my *shefela?*" he asked as they walked to the parlor for privacy.

"Oh, no." She smiled at him and squeezed his hand. "I wanted to speak with you about a job. I was thinking I could work with you at the Triangle."

He frowned and dropped her hand. "A job? Why? And why a factory?"

Her eyes widened and she stepped away from him. "Wait, what? You knew I worked in a factory. How do you think we survived all that time?"

Abraham swallowed hard as his thoughts raced. Where was this coming from? Of course he knew that. He hated himself for it.

"Yes, and you were amazingly strong to do so," he said, putting his hands on her shoulders. "But you don't need to be anymore. I'm here now."

"I want to be more than just the umbrella."

He tilted his head in confusion. She pulled away from his hold. "Useful when the rain came, when you needed me to keep my family safe to survive in Russia. But now you just want to toss me in the corner since you're back to be my sunshine?" She shook her head and looked at the floor. "That might work for our parents. But not for us."

She looked back to him. "Jeremiah wouldn't treat me that way."

He processed what she said for a moment. "You're right. I apologize." He tried to read her facial expression but found it inscrutable. He cleared his throat and proceeded with caution. "But what are you thinking? You're not planning to work forever, are you?"

"Of course not." She frowned. "But the crisis isn't over yet. Your family is still back there."

His heart leapt when he understood her meaning. His family was her family. He gathered her in his arms.

"Yes, my *shefela*. They are. And you are a tigress to care for them and sacrifice yourself this way."

She leaned her head on his shoulder. "It's what you do for family."

He pulled back to look down at her again. "Your Tatty will not be happy with this idea though."

"Because of Saturdays?"

He nodded and combed a hand through his hair.

"You work Saturdays."

"I'm not his daughter. And I have to."

Ruth narrowed her eyes. "But I have to also. We just discussed why my wages are also necessary."

He swallowed hard. Why couldn't she see what

she was asking? He was barely wrapping his head around her voluntarily going to work. It was one thing for a woman to work when she legitimately had no choice. But choosing to leave your duties at home to work alongside men? Giving up her role in preparing *Shabbat*? She had to know her father would see this as a direct insult.

He searched her face for any softening.

She held her chin up, resolute.

He finally raised his hands in surrender. "I'm on your side. But you know how traditional your father is. You'll still need to have this argument with him."

"Fine, I will." She turned and left the room.

He rubbed a hand over his face and sighed. Was it really only five minutes ago he'd felt those warm and fuzzy feelings about arriving home? One thing was certain, he had a lot to learn about women.

Ruth

Friday March 19th, 1909

736 Days Until the Fire

Tatty murmured the lines of the *Kiddush* blessing and passed around the wine glass. The *challah* lay before him on the table, covered by Momme's embroidered cloth. Ruth tried to quiet her churning mind to embrace the familiar ritual. She'd lit the candles with Momme and Ester in Russia, but they had not celebrated a full opening *Shabbat* ritual since Tatty left. Unspoken among them was that it almost seemed a betrayal. He'd been the traditional member of the family, the one they did it all for.

Tatty held to the "keep it" and "remember it" rules of *Shabbat*, tyrannically enforcing them. He abstained from the *Talmud's* thirty-nine forbidden activities, like carrying, burning, and writing, from sundown on Friday through sundown on Saturday, and strongly encouraged the rest of them to do so also. It was black and white to him; it was written, so it was done.

Ruth, however, never understood this deep-seated acceptance of the rules. To her they seemed like mere technicalities—an excuse for men to sit around arguing about logistics and interpretation. She especially found them to be fruitless in the face of the struggles they'd been forced to survive. How could you argue for sitting still and doing nothing when you're wondering how you'll provide your next meal?

Tatty finished the last lines of the *Kiddush* and picked up the *challah* to tear off a piece and pass it. Ruth's stomach grumbled at the signal for breaking bread to commence. Once the *challah* returned to Tatty, they raised their bowed heads to dig in.

"*A sheynem dank* for dinner," Tatty said and took a sip of wine. His elbow bumped Abraham's shoulder.

Abraham tried to move his chair to give Tatty

space, but with Ruth on his other side, there was none.

Ruth slid her plate and leaned away in her chair.

*"*Ya, *a sheynem dank,* Rachel,*"* Abraham's father, Samuel, spoke. "It's nice to have a woman around."

Momme blushed. "My pleasure, Samuel. You and Jacob work so hard peddling your wares all day. I only wish dear Sarah could be here to help spoil you all."

"She will be soon, God willing. Along with my *boychicks* and daughters." Samuel kissed his fingers and offered them to the air.

"God willing," Tatty echoed, wiping his mouth. "Is that *taiglach* I smell?"

"Ya, I made it Tatty," Ester said with a smile. "I found fresh honey for the dough at the market."

Tatty grinned. "My favorite. I can't remember the last time I had *taiglach*." He leaned over and nudged Samuel with his elbow. "We'll be needing our little *berryers* to let our pants out soon, eh?"

Ruth rolled her eyes and pushed her plate away. She didn't know why the references to their housekeeping abilities bothered her so. It had always been that way, but where was the remorse for leaving them? The pride in their survival?

All the men seemed to care about was having the women there to spoil them again.

"What's wrong with you?" Tatty frowned. "You and Abraham can't be fighting already."

Samuel laughed. "Wait until you're married for that *dreck*!"

Ruth looked up at the two of them laughing together and knew it was time. She had been rehearsing her argument for the Triangle since she and Abraham spoke, but was still dreading the conversation to come. Momme gave her a warning look and mouthed, "Not now."

Ruth averted her eyes from Momme and took a deep breath. "Tatty, I want to work at the Triangle Factory with Abraham."

"What?" Tatty asked. He looked to Abraham. "You told her no, of course, ya?"

"I said she had to speak with you," Abraham said.

Momme nudged Ester. The two stood and began clearing dishes.

"I am not his wife yet," Ruth said. "And I am perfectly capable of choosing how I spend my time. I feel the family would still benefit from me working. I provided for us in Russia, after all."

Tatty looked down at his hands in his lap. "You did what you had to, and God will forgive that. But you are here now. The men can provide for the family and continue to pool our money for Abraham's family's passage. Your role is to prepare for us to celebrate *Shabbat* together as a family each Saturday."

Ruth crossed her arms and leaned them forward onto the table. She focused her gaze on her father. "After you left, we couldn't afford the luxury of abstaining from all the forbidden activities of *Shabbat*. We lit the candles on Friday and moved on."

Samuel stood from the table and grabbed his coat. Silently, he opened the front door and slipped out.

Tatty crossed his arms, leaning forward onto the table as well. "I regret that. But what is done is done and God will forgive us. Here in New York, we can keep and remember the full rituals and spirit together."

She glanced down for a second before returning his icy stare. "How much is rent?"

Both Abraham and Tatty sputtered in shock.

"How dare you ask such a thing!" Tatty shouted.

"Ester, go into our bedroom and close the door," Momme barked.

Ester tried to catch Ruth's eye, but Ruth continued to stare down Tatty. Momme snapped a dish rag at her and she scurried into the other room. Momme turned her attention to scrubbing dishes in the wash basin.

"Does Momme know?" Ruth persisted. "We knew in Russia. We had to, because I was the one paying it. Both Ester and I were. And Momme took in sewing as well. Why shouldn't we know here? We're still contributing members of the household."

Tatty looked at Abraham for help.

Abraham shrugged and finally spoke. "Fifteen a month, Ruth. It's fifteen a month."

Tatty glared at him. But Abraham stared straight ahead and pretended not to notice.

"Thank you, Abraham." Ruth smiled. "So, fifteen a month, plus household expenses, plus saving to bring the rest of Abraham and Samuel's family over."

Tatty gave a small nod.

"Wouldn't it be best then, if I'm willing and able, to get additional pay to contribute?"

Abraham looked over at Ruth and back to Tatty. He cleared his throat. "It would help my family get here sooner. And it's not like I'm fully observing *Shabbat* anyway."

Ruth's heart swelled at Abraham's efforts to help her. She smiled at Abraham as he illustrated her point.

"And what of her safety?" Tatty grumbled.

"I will walk her to and from the factory each day. And I'll handle all dealings with the foreman for her," Abraham said.

"And for Ester," Ruth piped in.

"No!"

Tatty slammed his fist down on the table. "Absolutely not and that is final. The law says school is mandatory until fifteen. We follow the law. Ester will go to school for one more year."

Abraham took Ruth's hand in his own. "There are reasons they put this law into place to stop child labor in the factories. Please let this matter go, Ruth."

"But you'll support me working in the factory?"

"If you really want it." He squeezed her hand.

"And you, Tatty?" Ruth turned to her father.

Tatty hesitated a moment before speaking. "I appear to be powerless here. But mark my words, you give up traditions at your peril. One day you'll look back and not remember who you are."

Ruth jumped from her chair and ran over to her father to wrap her arms around him. She kissed him on the cheek. "Thank you!"

He waved a finger. "You must walk with Abraham every day and let him handle all dealings for you, *fershtay?*"

Ruth nodded, smiling.

"And only until Abraham's family arrives," Tatty

continued. "After that you will marry immediately and respectably manage affairs at home."

She nodded again.

Tatty patted Ruth on the cheek before standing.

"Abraham, walk with me. I'd like to speak with you further."

As Abraham stood to join her father, Ruth rushed over and grabbed his hands.

"Thank you for speaking on my behalf."

Abraham offered a strained smile. "This is new for me as well, Ruth. But I'm trying."

She grinned. "And I appreciate it."

Her father stood at the door, waiting with his coat.

Abraham joined him. They both touched the *mezuzah* and kissed their fingers as they left.

Ruth turned to her mother. "Well?"

"Well what?" Momme said while drying a dish.

"Aren't you proud of me?"

Momme picked up a dirty pot from the stove. "For what should I be proud?"

"For standing up for myself? Helping the family?"

"Oh, that was what that was?" Momme scratched at caked food in the pot with her fingernail. "I thought it was waging an unnecessary battle."

"Unnecessary? But I won! I got what I wanted."

"*Mazel tov.* At what expense?" Momme scrubbed at the spot with her wet rag.

Ruth started putting away the dried dishes. "What do you mean, at what expense? They both agreed without my giving up anything."

"Ah, that's not what I meant. I meant at what expense for them? Your father and Abraham are not your enemies, Ruth. You have much to learn about men before you marry."

"Abraham's fine with what happened. He said so." Ruth picked up a dry dish rag and twirled it between her hands.

"Because he is in love and knows that's what you want to hear. But what about what *he* wants? Can you understand they are worried? They weren't fighting against you to be mean. They've seen and experienced things you haven't." Momme handed the washed pot to Ruth to dry.

"As have I," Ruth said, jutting out her chin.

Ruth thought of the time she'd been forced to tackle a woman in the market to fight for the last rotten cabbage. She'd won. Now, she remembered the pride she'd felt as she brought it home to Ester and Momme. The heady rush she'd felt at being strong enough to survive. They'd dined for days on cabbage-flavored broth. Abraham and Tatty had never had to summon that strength here in America, where jobs were plentiful and wages were good.

Momme snatched another dirty pot from the stove. "I know you have. But it's not a competition. Relationships are a give and take. We share our wisdom and experiences and protect our loved ones. We also try to put ourselves in the other's shoes. Imagine why they might react a certain way."

"Exactly, Tatty should try to imagine my struggles in Russia. How they changed me. He should realize I'm no longer the naïve little girl he left."

"You're forgetting that Tatty didn't abandon you or leave you there on purpose. He was running for his life. He feels guilt about that. It will take him time to forgive himself. But the last four years were not easy for him either. He was alone. He had no family here to celebrate *Shabbat*." Momme turned to face Ruth and waved a soapy hand in her face. "And now we're finally here and you're telling him you don't want to celebrate with him."

Ruth hesitated before hanging the dry pot.

"But what about you, Momme? You faced an interrogation from the czar's soldiers and barely blinked. Yet Tatty won't even tell you what the rent is for the apartment? Don't you deserve more?"

Momme leaned over the sink to finish scrubbing the pot. "I don't want more. I enjoy caring for my husband and allowing him to care for me. I've missed that. Just being comfortable with our roles."

Ruth stood in silence, twisting the towel.

Momme passed the finished pot over to her. "You're no longer playing a card game in the parlor with your childhood friend. If you keep pushing to get your way and treating Abraham as your rival instead of your partner, you will end up unhappy, Ruth."

Momme dried her hands on her apron and walked to the bedroom door. She opened it and looked inside.

"Ester? You can come out now, *bubbala.*"

"Did they eat my *taiglach?*" Ester asked, running to the stove.

Momme came up behind her at the stove and stroked her hair. "No one really had an appetite for it tonight. But we can serve it tomorrow."

Ester stuck a finger into the center. "It will keep. Do you need help or can I read in the other room?"

"I've got it." Ruth picked up the last dirty pot.

Momme patted her arm and left with Ester.

As Ruth scrubbed she thought about Momme's

words. How could she think it was that simple? How could she just shelve all her emotions and experiences from the past four years and pretend they hadn't happened? Ruth didn't want to make Abraham a rival, but Momme was wrong to think that pushing would make her unhappy. Pretending nothing had changed and just returning to the way things were before would. As much as Ruth knew that's what they all expected, she knew she'd never be able to do it. She hoped her mother was wrong and Abraham wasn't just going along with things to make her happy. Because for their marriage to work, Abraham would have to see her for who she'd become, not who she was before.

A b r a h a m

Sunday March 21st, 1909

734 Days Until the Fire

Ruth would be fine, wouldn't she? Abraham sighed, unable to sleep. He turned to his other side, carefully avoiding the hot stove wedged next to the bed. He had enough burns from rubbing against it. Next to him, his father snorted and turned to the wall, disturbed by Abraham's movement. They'd performed this dance most of the night as Abraham tossed and turned. The bed was just too small.

    Ruth would be okay working at the factory. He'd

be there. She was strong and resourceful. And most of the stories were merely rumors. No one had actually seen a foreman act inappropriately. Still he worried. He was grateful Ruth wanted to bring in money to help his family come to America. But why did she need to work in a factory to get that money? Wasn't there some other way?

A piece of coal fell in the stove, startling him from his thoughts.

Next to him, his father turned to face him and stifled a yawn with the crook of his arm. "Why don't you go to the bathroom and clear your head?"

"I'm sorry, Abba, I just can't stop thinking."

"I know," Samuel said. "But you're going to break the bed with your tossing and turning. Go wear some grooves in the floor boards in the hall for a bit, and give my back a break, ya?"

"Yes, Abba."

Samuel waved him off and turned to the wall.

Abraham slipped out of the bed and winced as his feet touched the cold floor. He picked up the little kerosene lamp sitting on the kitchen table and turned the knob so a slight flicker of light appeared. He tiptoed and slowly opened the apartment door to step out to the landing. Shadows billowed on the wall as he walked with the lantern. A moth thudded against the glass and he waved it away with his hand.

Abraham didn't expect to see anyone at this time, so he was surprised to see the pregnant woman from down the hall step out from the bathroom. She stifled a shriek and reached for the wall to steady herself.

"So sorry, I didn't mean to startle you, Mrs..." He trailed off, realizing he didn't know her name. He'd seen her and her husband coming and going for months with their other two children, but never had an occasion to speak with them. How strange. Back in Russia he knew all their neighbors.

"No worry. It's Mrs. O'Leary. I met your women-folk yesterday. Best wishes by the way, Ruth's a dear."

He thanked her as she waddled back to her own apartment. Ah yes. The intricate network of women. He remembered walking into the cozy scenes of his mother laughing as she kneaded bread while a neighbor sat chatting over a cup of tea. Thinking back, almost every detail he knew about a neighbor or shopkeeper had been discovered and shared by one of his sisters or his mother. His chest ached with a pang of longing. He missed his mother and sisters and the larger community they had connected him to. It had been so long since he'd heard his mother's laughter.

The generosity of Ruth's offer suddenly hit him. She'd experienced factory life before— she knew what she was getting into at the Triangle. If anything, she'd experienced worse in Russia. But she was volunteering to sacrifice the comforts of home to return to a factory so his family could come sooner. A calmness descended upon him. Mrs. O'Leary was right. Ruth was a dear. He should be grateful.

He said a quick prayer thanking God for orchestrating the encounter with Mrs. O'Leary to provide this clarity. He tiptoed back into the apartment and slid back into the warm bed next to his father.

R u t h

"You ready?" Abraham asked.

Ruth nodded. "As I'll ever be." She looked up at the building towering over them. It stood at least ten stories high with arched windows and curving decorative stonework at the top. The Triangle Waist Company sign with its prominent dark black triangle logo marked the top three floors where the factory was located. A line of men and women crowded the front door, all trying to get in to start the day. Abraham took her hand and pushed his way to the front.

"We need time to talk to the foreman before the bell rings," he said over his shoulder.

Inside, the crowd separated into three different lines, two for the elevators and one for the stairs. One of the elevators dinged and opened its doors, and the line lunged forward. Abraham tugged on her hand and maneuvered their way into the car. Ruth gasped at the clang of the metal gate behind her.

The elevator operator smiled and pulled the lever.

"First day?" he asked in English. He said something else she couldn't understand.

She smiled in return and took in the elevator surroundings. Plush carpeting adorned the floor and gold handrails lined the car. The gate was made of gold as well. She'd never been in an elevator. Her stomach flipped as the elevator lurched to life. Her heart pounded and she stepped back into Abraham as she watched the elevator climb the floors. All that stood between her and the floors flashing by were two golden gates. How could a machine feel both so delicate and powerful at the same time?

The elevator came to an abrupt stop and the operator pulled open the gates. Ruth stepped forward eagerly, happy to get off the rickety contraption and excited to see the factory itself. She stopped dead. Despite the ornate ambience of the building and the elevator, the factory floor itself was utilitarian. The entire room was crammed with rows of machines going almost wall to wall. There weren't even aisles in between. Instead everyone walked in single file through the only pathway around the perimeter of the room. Ruth made a mental note to always use the wash room before beginning the day; getting back out after those workstations were filled would be impossible.

"Do you want to leave your things?" Abraham asked, gesturing to a room next to Ruth. She turned to see a steady stream of girls entering what appeared to be a changing area.

She shook her head. She wanted to ensure she had the job first.

Abraham led her around the perimeter of the room to an office area on the other side. Ruth peeked in the open door and saw the foreman sitting behind a large wooden desk piled high with papers.

Abraham knocked lightly on the door.

The man looked up with an annoyed expression.

Abraham stepped forward and cleared his throat before addressing the man in English. Ruth could only gleam small snatches of what he said. "Mr.

Grosevich, sir .... Ruth...."

Her head swirled at them speaking about her without her knowing what they were saying. It was both frustrating and unsettling.

Grosevich stood and rummaged through a pile of the papers on his desk as he responded in English.

Ruth felt her stomach clench at the sight of him. Mr. Grosevich was a big man with a heaving gut. His clothing pulled over his midsection and had sweat stains marking his underarms. He looked in need of a wash, with long greasy hair and a yellowish pallor. She felt his eyes travel over her, examining her up and down. She shifted her weight from foot to foot.

Grosevich's eyes sharpened. He stepped closer and Ruth smelled his sour breath as he leaned closer to her. "Does she speak English?"

Abraham shook his head. "Yiddish, sir."

Her ears flicked at the familiar word before Grosevich turned back to his desk, muttering more in English she couldn't understand.

Abraham broke out into a grin. "Thank you, sir!"

Abraham grabbed Ruth's hand and pulled her from the office.

"I have the job?" she asked.

"Essentially, " Abraham laughed. "He'd never

agree outright. He's giving you a trial, but you'll show him. Let's get you settled."

He escorted her to the changing room and waited outside while she found a spot for her things, then he walked her to her station. Not being acquainted with the women's machines himself, there was not much he could show her. She wondered if he could hear her pounding heart as he gave her arm a quick squeeze.

"I'm right over at the Cutter's Station by the window there, see?" he said, pointing. "I'll meet you by the changing room at the end of the day, ya?"

Ruth watched him maneuver his way back through the stream of girls arriving at their stations to get to his own spot by the window. At least she'd be able to "see" him throughout the day, she thought.

She wiped her sweaty hands on her skirt. This was it. She was on her own. Time to prove her worth. She examined the station and machine before her. There was a basket by her elbow piled high with cut fabric. Dotted lines around the edges marked where her stitches should go. It looked like they were meant to be sleeves. She dug through her basket to see where the rest of the garment was, but all she found was more sleeves. How would she complete her garment?

The girl sitting next to Ruth put a hand on her

arm. She said something in English.

Ruth shook her head. She pointed to her basket. "Where's the rest?" she asked in Yiddish. "How do I complete the shirt?"

The girl shook her head. "No," and repeated herself in English. She picked up her own basket and showed Ruth.

Ruth reached over and saw that the girl's basket was full of sleeves as well.

The girl pointed to herself and gestured to her right arm and then reached over to tap Ruth's left arm.

Ruth looked around at the other baskets from the girls surrounding her. Each basket contained a different cut pattern. Ruth nodded in understanding.

"Finishers," the girl said slowly, pointing to another group of girls sitting in the last row of machines closest to the windows. She mimed sewing and attaching two sleeves together.

"Finishers," Ruth repeated slowly, sampling the strange word. The best spot, Ruth thought. They must be the senior seamstresses.

Satisfied that Ruth understood, the girl turned back to her machine and settled into her work. Ruth examined her own machine, adjusting the needle and knobs. She was soon ready and laid out her first sleeve to begin. She stepped on the pedal and was soon lulled by the hum of the machine. At least this was familiar.

* * *

Ruth entered the changing room and collapsed on the bench. She'd survived the first day. Her eyes ached and her head felt cloudy from the swirl of different languages all day. The girls had gaily chattered while they worked. Although she knew she'd be unable to keep up or participate, she'd half-listened and tried to snatch at words or phrases where she could.

She was unaccustomed to chatting at work. It was forbidden to speak in the factory in Russia. Yet she found herself feeling lonelier and more isolated here. It was different when no one was able to pass the day in idle chit-chat; the silence became its own kind of camaraderie. Here, she felt like an outsider looking in.

A tall girl with dark brown hair and a mischievous smile burst into the dressing room. Ruth was astonished to see the girl wearing red lipstick and rouge. She surprised Ruth further by sitting next to her and putting an arm around her.

"Ruth! Here you are," she said in Yiddish. She pulled Ruth by the arm up to stand. "Abraham said you were beginning today. I'm Chayele. My brother,

Yankel, is good friends with Abraham. Come meet everyone and *schmooze* with us."

Despite Ruth's protests, Chayele dragged her over to a group of chattering girls in the corner of the dressing room by the windows.

"Meet Ruth, Abraham's fiancé." Chayele squeezed Ruth's arm like an old friend. "That's Zusa, Mirele, and Filomena."

Ruth gasped to see an olive-skinned, crucifix-wearing girl conversing so intimately with the Jewish girls. Was she Italian? She'd never met an Italian face-to-face before.

"*Shalom*, Ruth."

"Welcome."

"Hello." The girls all smiled and proceeded to launch a torrent of questions at her.

"Where are you living?"

"How long ago did you arrive?"

"Were you excited to see Abraham?"

Chayele interrupted the onslaught. "Girls, girls, I don't think she speaks English yet. And give her a chance to breathe," she laughed.

The others joined her in laughter while Ruth clutched at her coat and tried to quell the oncoming surge of panic. They were all dressed in the shirtwaist and skirt combos she had seen other women wearing, their hair piled high atop their heads in a strange style that looked like a waterfall of loose curls. She reached up and felt her own plaited braids and wondered how they made their hair behave that way.

"You're right off the boat, aren't you?" Zusa asked in Yiddish.

Ruth nodded. "We arrived last week."

Mirele noticed Ruth staring at their hair. She pointed to her hair and said in Yiddish, "It's called the Gibson Girl style. It's the current fashion. I could teach you how to do it."

Zusa gave a quick glance at Ruth's hand-stitched one-piece dress. "I can take you shopping after your first paycheck."

"And I'll teach you English," Filomena said.

Chayele patted Ruth's hand. "We'll make you one of our own. Come sit by us tomorrow."

"Grosevich put me on the other end of the line," Ruth protested.

Chayele winked. "Let me take care of that."

"Ruth?" Abraham called from outside the dressing room.

The girls giggled.

"Well, don't keep him waiting," Chayele

whispered. "It's already been four years."

The girls all giggled again.

Ruth blushed and slid on her coat. "*A sheynem dank,* Chayele."

"My pleasure. Now *gay avek,*" Chayele said making a shooing motion with her hands.

Ruth smiled and ran out to meet Abraham.

He stood outside the dressing room with his arms crossed. "I was starting to fear I'd need to send in a search party."

"I'm sorry," Ruth said. "I met the sister of one of your friends."

"Chayele," Abraham chuckled. "That explains it. That girl could talk the hind legs off a donkey."

He steered her to the line for the stairs and gestured for her to open her bag to be examined. "They fear people stealing scraps for sewing at home."

Ruth held her bag open wide as the guard poked through. Eventually he nodded, and they exited through the door to the stairs.

"Chayele seemed really nice. She introduced me to her friends as well. She said you were good friends with her brother?"

"Yankel," Abraham nodded. "He's good folk. He took me under his wing when I got here. Makes me get out and have some fun from time to time."

Ruth pondered that for a moment and considered Chayele's painted face. "She's not a—what do you call it? Floopsy, is she?"

Abraham laughed. "No, Chayele's not a floozy, though she might be the center of any party. She's just been here awhile and has embraced America."

"America encourages painted faces?"

Abraham tilted his head and thought before answering. "America encourages fun, at least in your free time. Not like in Russia where you just go to work and come home."

"How do you spend *your* free time?"

Abraham turned to face her with a twinkle in his eye. "All kinds of ways. Seeing performers singing in shows, going to the circus, heading out to Luna Park."

"What's Luna Park?"

"An amusement park in West Brighton Beach. You can ride a roller coaster and see recreations of villages from all over the world—it's amazing. I'll take you one weekend."

Ruth mulled over this new word, *weekend*. She had no clue what a roller coaster was, but it sounded exciting. Everything Abraham mentioned was foreign and strange. They'd sung as a family around the piano or even in the street with neighbors on holidays. But shows? Performers? These were novel ideas.

Abraham glanced over at her with a mischievous smile. "Still love running?"

Ruth smiled.

"Race you home!" he shouted and took off ahead.

"You *gonif*! You still cheat!" she shouted and took off after him.

His laughter floated back to her as she ran. The cityscape flew by as she weaved in and out of people on the sidewalk, some shouting insults in response. They rolled right off Ruth. Her exhaustion evaporated, the caress of cool air on her face sweeping away her lethargy. She dug deep to run faster, her competitive instincts kicking in. She'd never felt so happy and free.

E s t e r

P.S. 63. The bane of her existence. That, and the phrase *compulsory school attendance*. She'd begun the countdown to her fifteenth birthday five minutes into her first day in the classroom.

It wasn't that she disliked school exactly. In fact, growing up, Ester loved school. But it had been a long time since she attended. The schools closed in Russia during the Revolution four years ago, and she'd never returned. And much like everything here in America, school was different from what she expected.

Just walking up to P.S. 63, the intricate Gothic building with its looming towers, felt overwhelming. Back in Russia the building was so overcrowded they'd been crammed into smelly basement rooms lit by gas lamps. She'd felt like a mole, unable to distinguish day from night. But here she felt like an imposter attending classes in this posh building.

Each morning, she woke with tightness in her chest, imagining the day ahead. She didn't want to learn English or sit through lessons in hygiene and American foods. She felt lost and alone.

Ester had such high hopes for America and the family being reunited. But so far, she'd just been disappointed. Yes, the family was together and living under the same roof again. But in some ways, they felt even further apart, everyone focused on establishing their own lives: Tatty spending as much time as possible at the synagogue, Ruth going to work each day and sharing her spare moments with Abraham, Momme setting up the apartment to be perfect and seeking out sewing clients. She longed for the days back in Russia, when home still felt like a home, all of them gathered together.

Ester tried to focus her attention back on today's grammar lesson. She used her sleeve to erase her slate.

Around her, students squirmed in their seats with their hands held high, begging to share their answers. Why was she the only one having such difficulty?

The teacher, Miss Cohen, stopped next to her desk. "Miss Feldman? We haven't heard from you."

Ester froze mid-erasure. Her mind reeled as she reached for an answer. Miss Cohen tapped her cane to signal her impatience.

Ester cleared her throat, "The *shagetz?*"

"Tut, tut, English only," Miss Cohen said.

Ester closed her eyes and swallowed. Her mind was blank. Her neck grew hot and she could feel her classmates' stares. She blinked her eyes but couldn't keep the tears from trailing down her face. Miss Cohen turned away and called on another student.

"The boy skated," the girl answered proudly.

Ester stared at her hands, clasped in her lap, willing her tears to stop. The dismissal bell finally rang and Ester let out a sigh of relief. She gathered her books and prepared to go. The other students chattered and converged into small groups as they left the classroom. Ester moved to the door.

"Miss Feldman, a moment please?"

Ester forced herself to nod politely.

Miss Cohen waited until the room was empty

before sitting herself behind the big wooden desk. She started to speak in English, but stopped and switched to Yiddish.

"Quite frankly, Miss Feldman, I'm concerned. You've attended classes for almost two months and made little progress. Are you practicing at home?"

Ester thought of the chores waiting for her. She had to hold back a laugh at the thought of Momme slowing down enough to practice English.

"It's hard to find time or someone familiar with the language," Ester said.

Miss Cohen nodded. "I understand. Perhaps your other family members might try attending the night class offerings?"

Ester thought back to Ruth's original lackluster response to the idea of night classes. It would be nice to share something again with her sister in this new place. Since Ruth had reunited with Abraham and started work, Ester felt like she barely saw her.

"I'll mention it to my sister. I could encourage her to attend and practice with me," Ester said.

Miss Cohen gestured to the door. The meeting was dismissed.

Ester fluttered around the small kitchen, trying to hurry through dinner prep by doing two things at once.

"Ester, pay attention—you'll burn the tongue!" Momme scolded from the ironing board.

Ester dropped the knife she'd been using and flew back to the stove to lower the heat. She stirred the chopped tongue and onions in the pan and tried to ignore the charred bits.

The door opened and Abraham and Ruth entered.

"And she said, leave it undone," Ruth said, removing her scarf.

Abraham shook his head, "Chayele never ceases to amaze me. One day she'll either be out on her *tuchis* or running the factory."

Ester called out from the stove, "Leave what undone? What did Chayele do now?"

Ruth pulled out a chair and sank into it. "Sorry, Little Bird. I'm too tired to tell the story again now. I'll tell you later, promise."

Ester turned away to roll her eyes. That was becoming Ruth's standard response. And "later" would never come, of course. At this point, there could be an entire anthology of *Tales from Work Ester Will Never Hear*.

With a sigh of relief, Momme put the iron down

with a loud clank on the cooling plate.

"Done. Finally." She expertly folded the newly crisp sheet and laid it in the basket. "I'm going to rinse off before dinner."

She left the room and shut the door behind her. Ester took the pan off the burner and turned back to her chopping board. She chopped the rest of the vegetables, craning her head to glean any more of Ruth and Abraham's conversation. No attempt was made to further include her. She cleared her throat.

"Um, Ruth, have you given any thought to attending those English classes with me?"

Ruth groaned. "Ugh, Little Bird, I'm dead on my feet by the end of each day. The idea of sitting in a classroom... Sorry!"

Ester turned away to hide her trembling chin. "I understand. I just thought it was maybe something we could do together. My teacher is pushing me to attend for extra practice."

"You need practice? I could help," Abraham said as he swiped a carrot off the cutting board.

"Really?" Ester asked. "That would be great!"

"Sure," he said, crunching on the carrot.

He reached for another and Ruth swiped his hand away. "Save some for the rest of us!"

She looked to Ester. "Didn't that Hedy lady down the hall say she volunteered at the Educational Alliance teaching English classes? Maybe you could ask her. She'd probably have more time than poor Abraham has to spare."

Ester turned away to brush the carrots into the pot on the stove. By the time she turned back, Ruth and Abraham had retreated to the parlor. She sighed. Was she losing her sister? They'd been so close in Russia. She remembered her nearly fatal brush with the flu. Ruth had never left her side, hovering to cater to her every need. Where was that Ruth now?

* * *

Ester squared her shoulders and straightened her skirt before knocking on the door. She hated speaking with strangers, and Hedy was more intimidating than the average stranger. Her forthright attitude and tendency to speak her mind was terrifying.

The door flew open and Hedy stood there with her hair askew, flour on her right cheek and a child wailing by her feet.

Ester stepped backward. "Oh. Is this a bad time?"

"Of course not. Come on in," Hedy said, wiping her hands on her skirt. She stooped and picked up the wailing child from the floor and turned back to Ester with a laugh. "There is never a good time."

Ester trailed behind her and shut the door as Hedy provided the child with a piece of carrot.

As the child crunched it happily, Hedy put him back on the floor and picked up a rolling pin to roll out dough. She looked up to Ester with a smile. "So, *vus muchs da?* What's on your mind?"

Ester felt a flush creep up her neck as she imagined asking this woman for help. And yet, seeing Hedy disheveled in her own chaos made her less intimidating somehow. This woman was trudging through the day as best she could, just like Ester.

Ester wet her lips and moved closer to the counter where Hedy stood. "Ruth says you teach English classes at the community center. I was hoping you could maybe help me?"

Hedy tilted her head and thought for a moment before speaking. She took her flattened dough and began pressing it into a baking pan. "Why do you want to learn English?"

Ester blinked at the question. "Why wouldn't I? We need to in this new country."

Hedy placed her cut vegetables into her pie crust. "Do we? What language do you speak at home with your family? At the marketplace?"

"Yiddish," Ester said slowly. "But that won't always be an option, right?"

Hedy shrugged. "It depends what you want to do here. What kind of communication you need."

"But you're a teacher," Ester protested. "Shouldn't you be encouraging me to learn?"

Hedy added salt to her vegetables. Ester was surprised to see a sudden darkness in her eyes. "Back in Russia, I survived two *pogroms* cowering in a secret compartment under my floor. I spent my life being told I might die if I spoke Yiddish rather than Russian."

She covered her vegetables with the top layer of pie crust. "I finally found a smuggler to help me escape to America a few years back. When I got here, I was pressured by the Jews here to learn English. To abandon my past and 'embrace America' in order to get ahead, to survive. To make money! It broke my heart, to be told once again I couldn't speak my native tongue or be who I was." She stopped and tossed another carrot to the child on the floor.

"Are you saying it isn't necessary?" Ester asked.

Hedy smiled. "What do you want your life to look like here in America? Are you looking to make money, set up a business?"

Ester shook her head. "No, I..." She trailed off and thought. "I'd probably like to get married and have a family. Like I would have back home."

Hedy nodded. "There are groups here working to preserve Jewish culture. People who encourage us to speak Yiddish to our children. Keep it alive. Teach young folk about their Jewish roots." She turned and put her pie into the oven. "An entire generation of children here already who do not know how to speak Yiddish! Did you know that?"

Ester felt a pang in her stomach. The idea that her own child might not know the language she'd spoken her entire life. The language her family spoke. How could that even happen?

Hedy leaned in to Ester. "You mentioned before I'm a teacher. I am. But I view that as more than just teaching you English. I want to teach other things, too—I want folks to understand they have a choice. That our life here in America could be all *about* choice, if we make it so." She covered Ester's hand with her own. "Russia was about survival in the true sense of the word. But here in America, you have a say. Come to the Educational Alliance. I'll teach you English, but see what Jewish life in America can be."

Ester's head spun. This was way more than she

anticipated. She expected a few English lessons in Hedy's apartment after school. And yet, she was intrigued.

She nodded. "When should I come?"

Abraham

Thursday June 10th, 1909

652 Days Until the Fire

He loved the feeling of Ruth's arm crooked in his. He squeezed her hand and she smiled before continuing her story. He loved watching her as she spoke. She talked with her hands, using them to illustrate her emotions and add impact to her words. She fascinated him, every part of her so full of passion.

He still felt like he needed to soak in all parts of her, like he was playing catch-up for lost time. Had she always had that dimple when she smiled? He'd developed a classification system in his brain: Russian Ruth and New York Ruth. Like he was engaged to two separate people. New York Ruth couldn't stand stuffed cabbage, but Russian Ruth had loved it. His mind was constantly scrambling to meld the two.

He turned to her. "Do you remember that time we picked berries and had that contest? Who could cram the most in their mouth?"

She laughed, "Jeremiah won, didn't he? He had what, fifty?"

"I think it was forty-seven. But do you remember after, when he almost choked?"

She scrunched up her face. "Oh ya, when he was celebrating, waving his fists in the air like a *grois-halter!* He could be such a braggart. Good thing you had the sense to slam his back."

"Your face when that berry flew—" he laughed.

She hit his arm playfully. "It landed on my foot! Stained my shoe even! A gooey splotch that lasted till the shoe wore out."

Her voice trailed off and they stared into each other's eyes, afraid to break the moment. The street light switched on above, highlighting a glimmer of copper in her hair. He reached up to brush it away from her face. How was he this lucky?

He heard a loud cough behind him and whipped around. Their fathers sat on the front stoop smoking their pipes. Abraham felt a flush of heat creep up his neck. He and Ruth jerked away from each other.

Samuel and Jacob exchanged a look.

"Ruth, your mother needs your help," Jacob said.

Ruth and Abraham climbed the steps. As they reached for the front door, Samuel put a hand on Abraham's arm. "Not you. We need a word with you."

Ruth gave Abraham a shrug and whispered "Good luck." He watched as the door closed behind her and turned to face the fathers.

"Abraham," Samuel started.

"We've done nothing inappropriate," Abraham hurriedly interrupted.

"I should hope not," Jacob grumbled.

Samuel's eyes shifted between the two. "Don't worry, son." He cleared his throat. "We were not accusing you."

"Then..." Abraham took in their serious expressions and stern postures. "What have I done?"

Samuel gestured to the step. "Please sit."

Abraham sat next to him and brushed off his knees nervously. Samuel offered him his pipe. He shook his head and Samuel clamped it back between his teeth.

Jacob cleared his throat. "We're concerned about your ability to manage Ruth."

"Manage her?"

Samuel spoke. "We fear you're focusing on the fun of the courtship and have forgotten your role as her future husband."

"Riding that Witchy Wave thing at Luna Park. Taking her to see actors at that theater. Going out dancing. At *night*!" Jacob waved his pipe, his voice starting to rise. "I shudder to think of the corruption."

Abraham gritted his teeth. He should have seen this coming.

Samuel glanced between Jacob and Abraham and spoke again, "The role of husband requires balance. We need to show our wives they're cherished. But we must also guide them to be appropriate mothers for our children. We must shield and protect them so they can be models of virtue and respectability."

"You need to start laying down the law," Jacob interrupted.

Samuel shot Jacob a look and gestured for him to back off. He turned to Abraham. "We understand this is a unique situation. You're both excited. You've been separated for so long. And Ruth is getting accustomed to a new place."

"You must save our traditions," Jacob interrupted.

Samuel turned to Jacob. "Do you just want to

take over?"

Jacob shrugged and puffed on his pipe.

Samuel turned to Abraham. "Things are slipping away. You're not keeping *Shabbat*. What's next? Skipping High Holy Days? Not attending synagogue at all? Do you see where we're coming from?"

Emotions swirled inside Abraham. Could they be right? He tried to examine the truth in their words. He remembered growing up and his father sitting at the table surrounded by children with his mother at the stove. All his father had to do was raise his glass and his mother would rush over to refill it.

It was his brother, Mark, who'd introduced the word *patriarchy* to him. Mark had been the smartest person he knew. He'd always been open to reading and new ideas. It was Father Gapon who brought him over to the radical side, though, by slipping him illegal copies of philosophers like Kant and Reinhold. Mark consumed these books like a man gasping for air. He'd quote the philosophers and share his beliefs on the topics whenever he could get Abraham and Jeremiah to listen. Had some of these ideas wormed their way into Abraham's head—like questioning the role of the husband in marriage? But he had *hated* those radical ideas. What's more, he blamed them for killing his brother and friend. Why was it all so confusing?

Samuel put his hand on Abraham's shoulder. "She'll be the mother to your children, son. Think on the character you want her to instill in them."

Samuel patted his shoulder and got up with Jacob to go inside. Abraham remained on the stoop, staring at the fading sun as darkness descended. The steady flow of people streaming home had slowed to a trickle of stragglers casting shadows in the streetlamp's glow.

Abraham struggled to digest what his father and Jacob had said. Did women need male guidance to be successful mothers? He thought back to his own mother and her soft-spoken ways. She'd molded his character and led by example. He did not question Ruth's character or values, but could he be exposing her to American corruption?

There had to be a middle ground. A way to prepare his bride for motherhood without snuffing her spark and passion. They were in America after all. Everything here was new and uncharted. He'd just have to be like Yankel and others he knew. He'd have to find a way to blend what was with what could be.

Ruth

Ruth was amazed how settled she felt in this new life after just a few short months. She knew she had Chayele and the girls to thank for that. Each day she sat with them on the line and listened as they chatted and laughed. She liked this team approach; in the Russian factory, she'd felt isolated by the focus on individual output.

Each line had a quota of finished product to fulfill each day. At first, Ruth thought the expected number was extraordinarily high. But the equipment was modern and fast and the girls showed Ruth tricks to make them go even faster. On their line, Ruth was given right sleeves. Chayele, in charge of left, showed her how angling the sleeve to the right made it zip through the machine. Mirele showed her to double pedal as it got to the end to tighten her stitch, and Filomena taught her how to reload her thread in less than three seconds.

She tried to keep up as they gossiped about news from the neighborhood or girls from the factory. They spoke in a fast-paced mixture of Yiddish and English with Filomena occasionally contributing some flowery phrases in Italian to earn a laugh. Although Ruth was only able to keep up with a quarter of the conversation, she still felt like part of the group.

At the end of one Saturday shift, the girls cornered her in the dressing room.

"It's time, Ruth," Chayele said, clapping her hands. "You've been here a few months. Let's get you looking like an American girl."

Ruth nervously patted her plaited hair. She'd been studying the Gibson Girl styles all the girls wore, but still didn't feel ready to attempt pinning it up herself.

Chayele smiled. "Yankel spoke with Abraham, and he agreed to accompany us shopping tomorrow."

"And I'll come over tomorrow evening to teach you to pin up your hair," Mirele said, placing a Gibson Girl picture cut from a magazine into Ruth's hand.

Ruth studied the picture. In contrast to Ruth's tight and practical style, the Gibson Girl style was softer and loose-looking, like it might come undone at any moment. It framed the face, begging to be touched.

Ruth nodded dazedly and turned to go, knowing Abraham was waiting. Then, Filomena called out.

"Oh, I almost forgot. I wanted to lend you this." She pressed a book into Ruth's other hand. "It's called a dime novel. Read with a dictionary. Fun to read and will help you learn English."

Abraham was leaning on the wall of the building, waiting for her when she left the factory. He smiled as she stepped out onto the street. It was strange that although they worked on the same floor, they didn't see much of each other during the day. And at night they were always surrounded by family. Their walks to and from work had become their only private time.

Ruth ran to meet him. "Sorry I made you wait."

Abraham shrugged. "It wasn't too long. Do you

have your pay envelope? We can still get to the bank before closing."

He pushed himself off the wall, and they walked.

"I want to take out some money for the shopping trip tomorrow, though." She handed him the book and picture to hold while she reached into her pocket. "How much do you think I'll need?"

"Ah, the shopping trip. I want to talk to you."

"Oh?" Ruth looked up and handed her envelope to him. "Chayele said you'd already approved it."

"I did. I have no issue with the shopping trip itself. You need new clothes. But I think we need to lay down some ground rules."

"Ground rules?" Ruth frowned. "Like?"

He looked at the book she'd given him. "Like this." He held up the book. "Who gave this to you?"

"Filomena," Ruth said, grabbing it back. "She said it would help me learn English."

He slowed his pace. "Why do you even need to learn English? All we speak is Yiddish at home and around the neighborhood."

"For communicating in the factory. You even speak English there!" She twirled a tassel on her dress. "I only understand a quarter of what they're saying."

He stopped and turned to her, causing a vendor

pushing a cart to shout at him. His face softened. He cupped her chin. "You've only been here a few months. It's impressive you understand that already. You don't think you'll continue to learn more?"

Ruth shrugged. "Maybe. But Filomena said it would speed up my learning. And be fun to read."

Abraham resumed walking. "Why don't you attend those classes if you want to learn English?"

Ruth wrinkled her nose. "I hated school. I could never sit still."

Abraham chuckled. "Why isn't that surprising?"

"I really have no interest in learning English in a formal way like that. I think that's why the book interests me. I could learn it while being entertained."

They had arrived at the bank. Only men were allowed inside to deposit money, so Ruth was forced to wait outside on the stoop for Abraham to return.

"I took out two dollars for your shopping tomorrow," he said, sliding the folded money into his pocket when he came back out.

He looked both ways before crossing the busy street, pulling her by the hand when he saw a break. "So, back to our conversation. I hear what you're saying and I even understand. I too had difficulty sitting still in school. But it's different here."

"Obviously!" Ruth said, gesturing around them.

He looked away and his voice cracked. "No, I mean, there's more temptation for corruption. Like your friends…"

Ruth bristled. "My friends are *not* corrupt!"

"Sorry. Wrong word." He took a deep breath. "I mean—inappropriate."

Her shoulders tensed and she opened her mouth to speak, but he waved his hand. "Hear me out. Please."

She exhaled loudly. But she let him continue.

"They're different from you, Ruth. None of those girls is betrothed. And most of them don't even have family here."

"Why should that matter?"

He skirted around a woman arguing with a vendor. "They have different priorities. Zusa and Mirele are here without families. They live together in an apartment with three other girls from the factory. Chayele and her brother board with a family not far from us. They pay for rent and food, but other than that, their money is their own. They're not worrying about saving, so they can afford to buy the latest clothing or books. They go out to socialize on their free nights and Chayele, I know, even goes out courting with strange men."

Ruth blinked at this, shocked by the freedom he described.

His hands tightened on her shoulders. "Do you see now why it is not fitting for a betrothed woman like you to socialize with them too much? Imagine that *shiksa,* Filomena, giving you such a book!"

She looked at him, sizing him up, before cracking a wicked smile.

"So, what's in the book that is so inappropriate?"

He laughed awkwardly before taking her hand.

"Stories that should make a girl like you blush."

"Oh." Ruth felt her face grow hot as she pictured what he meant. She pulled her hand from his and instead tucked her arm into his and leaned in to him as he slowed their pace to a more leisurely stroll.

"Maybe you could ask Ester," he suggested.

"Huh? Ester?" Why was he mentioning her little sister in connection with romantic stories?

"For help with English. She has those lessons with Hedy. I'm sure they'd love to have you join them."

"Oh... I suppose. I'm just so tired when I get home. And I'd have even less time with you." She pictured their pleasant evenings working on puzzles or playing games together at the table after dinner. Although the family was around and often participating as well, she still enjoyed the time with him and didn't want to lose it.

He tilted his head while he thought. "We could try conversing only in English on our walks."

She nodded.

"But, I have another idea. And it's almost as fun as your friend's book," he said with a wink. "You'll have to wait until tonight, though. It's a surprise."

She grinned and squeezed his arm.

✳ ✳ ✳

Darkness was just falling later that evening. As Ruth and Abraham rounded the block, she noticed workers up and down the street reaching with long torches to light the street lamps. Entranced by the beauty of the dancing flames in the glass lamps, she watched until Abraham nudged her with his elbow.

He gestured to a sparkling fortress ahead of them. "See? This we can enjoy together. And practice English at the same time."

Ruth tried to soak in every detail of the brick-fronted theater. The front was lit by a large sign advertising five-cent shows. Posters of cowboys riding horses and men and women in romantic poses were affixed to the walls.

"Tickets! Tickets right here! Five cents apiece," shouted a man dressed in a striped suit and straw hat. "Looking for tickets, folks? Step right up."

She turned to Abraham, "What is this place?"

"It's called a nickelodeon. It plays moving pictures." He squeezed her hand and navigated her through the crowd to a ticket counter with glass windows encased in gold carvings.

"Two to *The Cowboy Millionaire,* please," he said in English.

As the attendant handed him the tickets, Abraham smiled at Ruth. "Next time you'll ask for the tickets."

She fidgeted with her dress and looked to the floor. She had yet to speak any English in public.

Jaunty piano music played as they walked inside a dark, crowded room filled with rows of wooden seats as far as her eye could see. Movement drew her eyes to a large screen with pictures above the stage. She jumped as the picture changed to a close-up of a woman's face. It was huge! Like a color-less, flickering monster! Abraham nudged her in the back and guided her to two seats near the middle.

People mumbled as Abraham and Ruth stepped

over them and shuffled past their feet. Once settled, Ruth perched on the edge of her seat, swiveling her head to take in every detail. Abraham scrunched down low to rest his head against the back of his seat.

She searched for the source of the music and discovered a man playing a piano beneath a stage in the front. The music appeared to match the emotions of the film. Cards with English words flashed in between the action. Abraham told her they were meant to be narrating what was happening. He leaned over in the beginning to read them to her, but the people sitting behind them hissed at him to be quiet.

Ruth found she could follow the story even without words. She watched as a cowboy and a woman fell in love. But the cowboy lied to the woman, and she fled back to England. He followed her and won her back. By the end of the movie, Ruth was wiping away tears. She looked over to find Abraham looking at her.

"You liked it?"

She nodded. "It was beautiful. Like magical pictures coming to life."

He smiled. "That's how I felt the first time too."

As they made their way home, Ruth found her thoughts wandering to all she'd seen in America so far.

She looked up to find Abraham darting a glance at her.

"What are you thinking about?" he asked.

She sighed. "Just how wonderful everything is."

"Oh?" He tilted his head.

"America is just so different. So free!" She shook her head. "We earn enough to buy new clothes. See a magical moving picture. It's wonderful. Everything's wonderful. I just love it here!"

Abraham smiled. "I'm glad to see you're happy."

"Did you see the dresses the woman wore in the picture? I wish I could have a dress like that!"

He opened his mouth to say something and then shook his head, changing his mind. They walked in silence for a few minutes before Abraham spoke again.

"I invited Ester to come shopping with us tomorrow. I figured she needs new clothes as well, and she doesn't seem to have made many friends yet."

"Oh Abraham! I should have thought of that." Ruth put a hand on his arm. "Ya, she would enjoy coming. *A sheynem dank* for looking out for her."

"My pleasure. I enjoy being needed." He smiled.

Ruth tucked her arm in his and they continued their walk home.

E s t e r

"Beautiful! That skirt is a definite keeper!" Chayele gushed. She linked arms with Ester in front of the tall, glistening mirror and drew her close. "Ester, once we're done with you, boys will be *begging* to court you. You'll nab yourself a husband in no time!"

"Don't condemn the poor girl so early on." Zusa waved Chayele away from Ester. "Don't listen to her, you have plenty of time before settling down. It's a new world, *bubbele.*" She plopped a hat on Ester's head and tucked her hair. "A fine hat is the marking of any true American girl."

Ester gaped at her reflection in the mirror—at the stranger staring back at her. Gluttonous racks of clothing stood sentinel behind her. Panic bubbled in her chest at all this newness; the room swirled. Ruth, seeing Ester's panicked expression, stepped in and moved Zusa aside. Ester clung to her, digging her fingernails into Ruth's arm.

Ruth bit back a yelp and cleared her throat. "We're just here for new clothes today. No advice on life yet, ya?" She patted Ester's hand.

"Ach, where's the fun in that? Didn't you say your sister loved to learn?" Chayele said with a wink.

Ester shifted from one foot to the next.

Zusa looked from Chayele to Ruth and then leaned in to Ester. "How about we just start with new skirts and shirtwaists?"

Ester glanced at Ruth, who shooed her in the direction of the changing room. She forced her feet to move. The girls, armed with skirts and shirtwaists in different colors and patterns, descended around her. Ruth sat down on a bench in the corner.

I should have stayed home, Ester thought. But she'd been so excited when Abraham asked her to

98

join the shopping trip. It was the first time she'd been included since they arrived. That was the curse of being the quiet one—she often got overlooked.

Strange how she now wished they wouldn't pay quite so much attention to her. Unaccustomed to scrutiny, she found the girls' enthusiasm a bit oppressive. Peeking around the fitting room curtain, she sighed with relief. The hoards had finally moved on to Ruth's dressing room. She stepped out of the stiff, snug-fitting skirt they insisted she try and slid back into her well-worn, formless dress. Fashion was overrated. She'd rather stick out as the foreigner and be comfortable than feel trapped in modern garments all day. Ruth would force her to get them, though. Her sister always believed she knew best.

She folded the skirts and shirtwaists the girls had gathered for her and tiptoed from the fitting room. She'd leave them by the register and escape while they were occupied. She needed a moment to breathe.

She stepped outside and saw Abraham sitting on the stoop, carving an animal figurine. He looked up in surprise as she sat down next to him.

"Done already? Where's Ruth?"

"She's still trying things on," Ester said, smoothing out her skirt. The cold from the stone spread through the backs of her legs. "I just needed to escape for a moment. They're a bit..."

Abraham chuckled. "Loud? Intrusive?"

Ester laughed. "I was going to say overwhelming. But yes. I don't know how Ruth handles them every day. I'd go nuts."

"They mean well," Abraham said as he returned to his carving. "Chayele in particular has a heart of gold. She and her brother really took me under their wing when I first arrived. Friends make a big difference in a new world." He looked over at her. "Have you tried socializing with anyone from school?"

Ester shook her head.

"It might help," he said gently, brushing off a piece of wood from his carving.

Ester looked to the ground. "I didn't have many friends back home either. I had your sisters, but really all I've ever needed was Ruth and Momme."

Abraham was quiet in response, appearing to be focused on his carving. Ester looked at the animal shape emerging. Was it a bear?

"Family will always be blood. But remember, it's friends who sometimes really know you and help you see the truth about yourself."

Ester nodded like she understood. But in truth

she had no idea what he meant. How could a friend know her better than her family?

The door opened and Ruth stuck her head outside.

"There you are, Bird. We were wondering where you snuck off to. Abraham, I need a bit more to settle up." Her eyes drifted to Ester.

Ester blushed, thinking of the clothing she'd probably never wear that Abraham was paying for himself. A twinge of guilt cramped her stomach.

He stood and brushed off his pants. As he stuck his carving and knife in his back pocket, he gave Ester a wink. "Remember what I said, ya?"

He pushed open the door to join Ruth inside.

They returned a few minutes later, and Ester followed Ruth and Abraham as they set off for home. Once again, she was the one trailing behind, the tagalong. First she wanted less attention, now she wanted more. What was wrong with her? But it had been so cozy sitting with Abraham on the steps.

She watched Abraham bump his shoulder into Ruth's. "So, how was it?" He gestured to all the bags he was holding. "Did you get everything you need?"

Ruth smiled up at him. "I finally feel like an American. I got two shirtwaists and skirts, and Zusa is coming over later to teach me how to pin up my hair."

Abraham wrinkled his nose. "Pin your hair? Into that ugly curl-flowy-thing the girls are wearing?"

"It's not ugly!" Ruth said as she hit his arm. "It's called the Gibson Girl. And it's modern. Right, Ester?" Ruth called over her shoulder. "Aren't you excited to learn how to wear it?"

"Eh," Ester shrugged. "Those curls look complicated."

"I just think a bird might get confused and nest on your head," Abraham said with a laugh.

Ester put a hand over her mouth and giggled.

Ruth scowled. "You think that's funny? *The American hairstyle is funny?* Ester, didn't you appreciate the girls taking time to include you today?"

"Of course. What does that have to do with anything?"

Ruth said nothing.

"You're angry because I don't like a hairstyle?" Ester asked.

Ruth turned on her heel and stormed ahead.

Ester looked at Abraham in confusion. He shrugged and called Ruth's name, but she didn't stop.

"Ruth?"

Ruth looked up from where she sat knitting on the lumpy couch in the parlor. Ester stood in the doorway, afraid to step any farther.

Ruth bit back a sigh, patted the couch cushion next to her and shoved her knitting aside. Ester scurried over and dove onto the couch. She sat back up to smooth out her new skirt while Ruth turned to face her. They sat in awkward silence, each waiting for the other to begin. Finally, Ester took a deep breath.

"I'm sorry, Ruth. I don't know what I did to upset you, but I'm very grateful the girls took me out today."

Ruth softened. "Oh, Bird, no, I'm sorry I shouted at you. You did nothing wrong."

"Why were you so upset?"

Ruth chewed her lip. "I don't know, actually. I just felt overwhelmed, I guess."

"You? Why? Everything is going so well for you. I'm the one who doesn't fit in anywhere."

"What do you mean you don't fit in anywhere?"

Ester blinked back tears and felt her chin quiver. "I'm too young to work in the factory, and school makes me feel old and stupid. Most of the students are younger, but they all seem to know more. They're almost speaking fluent English while I'm still identifying pictures of a cat and dog."

"Oh, Ester." Ruth pulled her into a hug. "They've just been here longer. I feel the same way at the factory when the girls are all speaking around me. We have to be patient. We'll fit in eventually."

Ester looked up at Ruth and sniffled. "But that's it. I don't want to. I don't *want* to change my hair or clothing or learn a new language. I just miss home."

Ruth shook her head and frowned. "Have you forgotten what it was like back home? We were starving. It was dangerous—"

Ester waved her hand. "I'm not talking about that. I mean before. When we were all still together. Knew what was expected."

"What do you mean?"

"Well, you grew up knowing you'd marry Abraham and care for his home. I would have married his brother, Benyamin. Things were... simpler."

Ruth chewed her lip. "Yes, but we also had very little choice in the matter. Tatty and the men did all the decision making for us." She squeezed Ester's arm. "Think of the freedom you can have here. I am bound by my betrothal and what's considered appropriate for me. But you—you'll get to experience everything. Look at Chayele and the others! They go out without escorts, dress as they please, read what they want to and most importantly, they'll choose who they marry. They can marry for love and so can you."

"Don't you love Abraham?" Ester asked.

Ruth swallowed. "I feel closer to him every day. But we're still getting to know each other. We have history and respect each other. Love will grow."

"Like Momme and Tatty. They definitely love each other and their marriage was arranged."

Ruth ran a hand through her hair. "Ya, and that's exactly what I hope for. But choice is a powerful thing, Ester. Abraham and I are lucky, but you don't have to rely on luck."

Ester was quiet for a moment. Her head spun as she processed Ruth's words. Was Ruth right? Was the freedom of choice a gift? She thought back to that moment in the dress shop earlier and the closed-in feeling she'd felt as the girls discussed her future.

She shook her head. "With choice also comes responsibility. I'm not sure I *want* that burden."

"So, what, you just won't marry?"

"Nothing says I can't still have Tatty arrange a marriage for me, and Benyamin will be joining us here with the rest of Abraham's family eventually."

Ruth's jaw dropped. "You'd have Tatty arrange

your marriage?"

Ester shrugged. "I'm not making any decisions tonight. But you did say it's my choice, right?"

Ruth shook her head and picked up her knitting again to signal she was done with the conversation. Ester watched her.

"I'm sorry that disappoints you, Ruth."

She stood and left the room again while Ruth continued knitting.

Ruth

Ruth lifted her arms to air out her armpits. Her blouse stuck to her skin with sweat. Between the heat from the machines and the temperature of the day, it was sweltering in the factory. She glanced at the clock. Only ten minutes had passed since she last checked.

She stifled a yawn and grabbed another sleeve to feed her machine. She'd barely slept last night. It was that in-between season when it was no longer warm enough to sleep on the roof, but the air in the apartment was muggy and stifling.

Grosevich came up and clapped a heavy hand on

her shoulder.

"You." His breath smelled like onions and whiskey. He gestured for Ruth to follow him.

He seemed to want her to switch her seat to another table, the one with the finishing machines. Was this a promotion?

Filomena and Mirele exchanged a look. Chayele caught Ruth's hand and murmured "Don't go."

Ruth chuckled awkwardly. Was Chayele giving her a warning of some kind or did she not want Ruth to move because they'd miss her?

Ruth opened her mouth to ask, but Grosevich cleared his throat. She gave Chayele a shrug and scurried down to where he waited.

Grosevich sniffled and wiped his nose on his hand before speaking in rapid Yiddish. "A girl didn't show today. I'm putting you there to take her place."

Ruth smiled. The finishing machines were a coveted position. It would mean a promotion. She'd make two more dollars a week.

"Thank you, sir."

He looked at her with red-rimmed, glassy eyes. "Don't screw it up. No pay for imperfect pieces."

She nodded and slid into the empty seat. She was excited by this prospect, but she couldn't ignore the knot in her stomach. Why her? What if this was a mistake?

She greeted the other girls on the finishing line, but no one raised their eyes to look at her. Grosevich plopped down a pile of assembled shirtwaists held together by pins and was gone before she could even ask for instructions.

She leaned to a girl nearby. "A lot of work, ya?"

The girl did not respond.

Ruth repeated her statement in English, but the girl said nothing.

Sighing, Ruth picked up a shirtwaist, removed the pins and fed it through the machine. She looked to her old seat where Filomena was speaking. Her workday would be lonelier, but two dollars more a week would bring Abraham's family to America sooner.

* * *

Chayele burst into the dressing room. "How could you let him move you! Didn't you hear my warning?"

Ruth shook her head. "I'm sorry I moved. But if it means two more dollars—"

Filomena came up beside Chayele. "It's a trick."

"What kind of trick?"

Chayele sighed. "He goes for the inexperienced

girls and moves them to get free labor."

"Inexperienced?" Ruth put her hands on her hips. "I worked for years in the factories back in Russia."

"Of course you did, Ruth." Zusa put her hand on Ruth's arm. "She isn't saying you're inexperienced in skill, just in the workings of this factory."

Ruth shook Zusa's hand free and stepped back. "You make it sound like I'm some kind of *schnook,* just waiting to be duped."

Chayele crossed her arms. "Stop being insulted and listen! Did he say you'd get the two-dollar raise?"

Ruth thought back to her exchange with Grosevich. "Well, no," she admitted. "But everyone knows the finishers get ten a week."

Filomena shook her head. "Nothing should be assumed at the Triangle, Ruth."

Ruth felt a tide of anger surge inside her at Filomena and Zusa's pitying looks and Chayele's know-it-all attitude. She'd been at the Triangle six months now. Was it so impossible to believe the foreman had recognized her talent in that time and she'd earned this privilege?

Ruth raised her chin. "You're just jealous. All of you. You're mad he picked me."

Chayele gave a bitter laugh. "You wish!" She

turned to the door and the others followed.

Seething, Ruth followed. Usually they all walked home together, but today Chayele and the girls started toward home while Ruth strode over to Abraham. Yankel looked confusedly as the girls left him behind. He tipped his hat at Ruth and ran to follow them.

"What happened?" Abraham asked.

"Ugh," Ruth groaned. "They're mad that I'm better at my job than them."

Abraham scratched his nose and tilted his head. "Did they actually say that?"

"They got angry that Grosevich moved me to the finishing table. Can you imagine? Instead of congratulating me, they insulted me!"

"You let him move you?" Abraham asked.

"Not you, too!" Ruth glared at him.

Abraham held up his hands. "I'm sorry. Congratulations."

But as they started walking home, he brought up the topic again. "I have nothing but faith in you, Ruth. If Grosevich moved you, I hope it's because he recognized your talent and intends to make you a finisher. But don't lose your friends over it." He hesitated. "I don't know much about doings on the girls' side of the room, or how Grosevich treats them. But your friends have some experience. Maybe think on what they said and proceed with caution."

He patted her hand to soften his words and Ruth chewed on her lower lip.

* * *

"Where did this come from? We can't afford good slices of meat like this." Tatty slammed his plate on the table and glared at Momme.

Ester and Ruth exchanged a strained look. They tried to talk some reason into Momme. But in her excitement about Ruth's promotion, she'd gone a bit overboard, sending Ester to the market to get the best slices of beef offered, and setting the table with the good tablecloth and candlesticks.

"We're celebrating tonight, Jacob." Momme folded her hands in front of her and smiled. "We've been here six months, and Ruth got a promotion today. We need to embrace the joy in our lives for once."

Tatty scowled looking down at the six plates of meat. He opened his mouth to respond when Samuel clapped a hand on his shoulder.

"You're right, Rachel. And this *alter cocker* realizes as well. His stubborn nature has temporarily blinded him." He squeezed Tatty's shoulder, making Tatty wince. "We should have had a celebration when you ladies arrived. But we'll make up for it now, ya?"

Momme tilted her head waiting for Tatty's response.

Tatty looked between Samuel and Momme. Finally he chuckled and shook his head. "Ya, Samuel. Thank you for pointing out my shortcomings. But if we're going to make this a real celebration, Abraham needs to grab the *Manischewitz* from the cabinet."

The women breathed a sigh of relief as Abraham stood to get the wine. He poured glasses, and Tatty lifted his in a toast. "*L'chaim.*"

They clinked glasses and took a sip and then Momme said, "And to family being together. My heart feels like it's beating again."

Samuel leapt out of his seat and scrambled to his bed, where he pulled his violin case from underneath.

"Let's make this a real celebration!" He took out the violin and played a note. His face took on a peaceful expression. "It's been far too long since I've played for joyful reasons."

He tightened the strings and soon a foot-tapping

melody enveloped them all. Tatty got to his feet and held out his hand for Momme to join him. She smiled and put down her napkin. Moments later, their steps naturally synchronized, they were twirling around the room and her eyes sparkled. As Ruth watched, it brought her back to the night, years ago in St. Petersburg, when the country-wide strike that had caused so much hardship finally ended.

They'd been huddled together in Momme's bed for warmth, telling stories to try and distract each other from their hunger. Momme was in the middle of an old favorite from her childhood about a boy and a goat when they heard cheers in the street. Momme broke off mid-sentence.

"What's that?" Springing out of bed, they ran to the window. Their few remaining neighbors stood in the street hugging and laughing while others carried tables and chairs out from houses. Mrs. Abramovich and Mrs. Aleshkovsky from down the block were passing out glasses, which their husbands filled with vodka. Momme grabbed her shawl and ran to the front door with Ruth and Ester quick on her heels.

"What happened?" Momme asked the first person she saw.

"The czar agreed to a Parliament. He's giving us a voice!"

Momme gasped. "Does that mean—"

"The strike is over!" Old Man Lashevich shouted. "Still a long road to go. Knowing the czar, he'll change his mind again. But tonight, we celebrate."

Someone picked up a violin and began to play. Soon he was joined by a harmonica and two boys banging on pails. Dancers flocked to the area in front of the makeshift band.

Momme grabbed Ruth and Ester's hands and twirled them into the crowd. As they squealed with joy, the deep worry lines on Momme's face seemed to disappear. Her laughter echoed in the cool night air as she hiked up her skirts and danced as if, for one night, she had not a care in the world.

In this cozy apartment in New York, that memory felt like it belonged to a different life. The worry and troubles they experienced when the czar *did* go back on his word six months later no longer mattered. They were finally safe. Tonight's joy could be real.

Dancing tonight had the same effect on

Momme's face; Ruth marveled at how young her mother looked. How young her mother really *was*, Ruth realized. It dawned on Ruth that Momme had had two children by the time she was Ruth's age—Jeremiah and herself. Ruth exhaled a deep breath, startled at the thought.

Abraham's voice interrupted her. "Care to dance*?"*

She smiled. "Of course."

Abraham's hand tightened on hers as he helped her to her feet. They clasped hands and took three tentative steps forward, swinging their hands between them. Then they moved backwards, ending back-to-back. As they stepped to travel for the next part, his foot tangled with hers and they tripped.

He laughed. "I guess they have a few years on us to make it look easy, huh?"

She glanced at her parents, who appeared lost in their own world. They seemed able to anticipate the other's next movement before it was even made. She rubbed her foot and looked up at Abraham. He tilted his head, inquiring if she wanted to try again. She took his hand, and they took another hesitant step together. This time they moved without disaster. Slowly, they made their way around the room, feeling for the slight lean of the body or change in breathing the other made. Their movements blended and felt natural. Thrilled, Ruth tilted her head back and laughed.

Was this what was meant to happen for them? A blending of movements as they came together to become one? She wondered how her life would have been different if they hadn't been separated four years ago. She'd have married as early as Momme—Tatty and Samuel had already been arranging her wedding to Abraham when they left Russia. She'd be a wife for over four years by now. Probably a mother as well.

She imagined her life in a world where no turmoil had come to Russia. There would have been no protests for Jeremiah and Abraham to join. But she'd be sheltered and dependent on Abraham for everything, never knowing the pride of bringing home a pay envelope and contributing to the household. Nor would she have felt the weight of fighting for her family's survival, nor the excitement of coming to America and discovering what it was like to celebrate a promotion or laugh with friends while working.

That horrible day four years ago robbed her of her brother and separated her family. But maybe God had a plan. Maybe she was meant to experience those struggles in order to change her future. The challenge now would be learning to blend and balance her experiences with Abraham's.

"What are you smiling about? It looks like your mind's whirling." Abraham squeezed her hand.

She laughed. "I'm just happy."

He smiled. "I hope I can always make you happy."

He leaned over and kissed her on the forehead and held her tighter as they continued to twirl together. Ruth noticed Ester sitting at the table watching them. She smiled at Ester before leaning her head down to rest on Abraham's shoulder.

R u t h

546 Days Until the Fire

Ruth smiled as she finished the stitches on her last blouse of the day. She turned to crack her back in the chair the way Chayele had taught her. It was pay day. Soon all the tension from the past week would be worth it. She allowed herself a quick glance over to where Chayele, Mirele, Filomena and Zusa sat enjoying themselves. They still hadn't spoken to her since the fight in the dressing room. Hurt by their laughter, she frowned and looked away.

Her gaze settled on the kindergarten corner in the back of the room. It was nicknamed as a joke for the youngest girls in the factory, who worked there trimming extraneous threads. It was said none of the girls was younger than thirteen, but she wondered if the factory was truly obeying the child labor laws Tatty spoke about. Since most of the young girls were brand new to the country, she guessed it was difficult to verify their ages.

Truthfully, she didn't understand all the fuss about the age requirement. She and Ester had both worked back in Russia when they were younger than thirteen. She didn't feel they'd suffered for it. But school was also required longer here than back in Russia.

To stay in school longer—to really feel comfortable reading and writing—would have been nice, she had to admit. Although Ester still complained about school, she was improving each day with her English language and writing, and Ruth was proud of her. Abraham sat with her some nights to help her sound out words from the newspaper.

Ruth had given up hope of being much of a reader herself, at least of English. But she was pleased to anticipate how her and Abraham's children would benefit from an American education.

Grosevich strode over to the kindergarten corner to hand out pay envelopes. He bent close to one of the smallest girls. With a sly smile, he lifted a strand of her golden hair and pushed it behind her ear with one stubby finger. She flushed and her body tensed. The girls around her kept their heads bowed, focused on their trimming. Ruth's stomach heaved as she looked away. Had anyone else seen this? The steady drum of machines continued, interspersed with chatter and laughter. It seemed his gesture had gone unnoticed.

He continued his distribution and made his way to Ruth's line of machines. The girls surrounding Ruth began packing up their work.

"You." He pointed to her. "No pay for training."

He moved on to the next girl.

Ruth grabbed his arm. "Training? You never said this was training. And what about my usual pay?"

He shrugged. "You didn't do your usual job."

Ruth sat there in shock. Two of the other girls exchanged looks and leaned together, whispering.

"Has he done this before?" Ruth asked.

They stood up, the noise of their scraping chairs on the floor drowning out their whispered voices.

"Has he?" Ruth shouted.

One girl turned back and spoke in Yiddish. "It's a game he plays. When he needs extra hands, he pulls someone up temporarily."

Ruth held back tears. "Why didn't you tell me?"

The girl shrugged and turned her attention back to her friend as they moved to the dressing room.

With all the pay envelopes now distributed, the floor erupted into chaos. Chairs scraped back, and a steady stream of girls moved as one, chattering about plans for their free day.

Ruth looked up to find Chayele and Filomena standing in front of her. "We tried to warn you."

"I let my pride blind me."

Chayele pursed her lips. "Come on, you can't sit there moping. They pulled one over on you this time. You'll come back Monday to your old position and be the wiser for next time."

The girls waited while Ruth gathered her belongings. She stopped to sniffle and wipe her eyes a few times, and they ended up being the last ones to leave. Filomena squeezed her hand while the guards checked their bags at the door. Mirele patted her on the back as they walked down the stairs. When they emerged onto the street, Ruth spotted Abraham deep in conversation with Yankel, so she crossed her arms and leaned on the wall to wait. But Chayele pushed in between the boys.

She gestured to Ruth. "Your girl got snookered."

Then she led the rest of the group away, leaving Ruth and Abraham alone.

Ruth blinked back tears and tilted her head up to look at him. But instead of stepping closer to her like she expected, he looked away, not meeting her eye.

"I know you warned me." She shook with emotion and gestured with her hand wildly. "That's what you want to say, isn't it? That you told me so?"

He stuck his hands in his pockets. "I was afraid this was going to happen. But you got so defensive."

"And you all just accept it?" She balled up her hands into fists at her sides. "How does the factory get away with doing this?"

He shrugged. "They're the best factory in the city. They're never seeking out employees, Ruth."

"That doesn't give them the right to completely take advantage of us." She grabbed the door. "I'm not giving in yet. I can't go home to face Momme without at least telling her I *tried* to get my pay."

She took the stairs two at a time before he could stop her. She heard the door slam closed and his footsteps echoing behind her, but she didn't stop.

It was dark as she reached the ninth-floor landing, except for a lone light shining in the office at the back of the floor. As she crossed the dark room, she heard the faint sounds of a scuffle and a stifled scream. It was coming from the office. Stopping in her tracks, she wondered if she should wait for Abraham.

There was a shrill shriek followed by sobbing.

Ruth sprinted across the factory floor, her feet moving without her even realizing it. She reached the office door and stopped in horror. Grosevich was holding down the golden-haired girl from the kindergarten corner with one hand, while his other roamed under her skirt. The girl's cheek was streaked red with a bloody gash, and her blouse was torn.

"What are you doing?" Ruth shouted.

Grosevich spun to gape at Ruth as he pushed the girl away. Taking advantage of his distraction, she scurried out the office door and clattered down the stairs. Abraham's footsteps pounded on the empty factory floor as he ran up behind Ruth.

Grabbing her arm, he dragged her away without a word. She froze in the stairwell as she realized what she had just seen.

"We can't stop here. It's not safe." Abraham dragged her down the stairs.

They emerged on the street, where streetlights were being lit as dusk descended. Abraham led her across the street and down a quiet side street before he finally stopped. She stood in shock for a moment before looking up at him.

"That girl. She's a child..." She trailed off.

Abraham shrugged his shoulders helplessly. "I told you it wasn't all perfect."

She tore her gaze away from him and looked at the city surrounding them. A few dirty boys scampered along the busy street. She watched as one stopped and grabbed a wallet from a distracted man's pocket while he inquired about a shoe shining. Suddenly, she saw the mud and sewage in the gutter ahead of her and smelled the rotting food that had sat in the sun all day at the market behind her.

"I've been blind," she said.

"You escaped a revolution." He squeezed her hand. "It's different here. The rot's more buried."

Her breath tightened in her chest. She let the tears erupt and Abraham wrapped his arms around her. She leaned her face into his shoulder and let him hold her while she sobbed.

Ester

Ester woke in a cold sweat. A nightmare? She groaned as she heard Samuel's snores—at least, she guessed they were his, though perhaps they were Tatty's—loud even through the wall. She cautiously turned onto her side. She and Ruth found it easier to sleep head to foot, which seemed to give them more room. But that meant she sometimes ended up with Ruth's feet in her face. As Ester stared at Ruth's foot, trying to will herself back to sleep, she realized she had a full bladder.

Ugh, she'd give anything for a chamber pot right now. But Tatty refused to allow anything as archaic as a chamber pot in the apartment. He was enamored with the modern conveniences of America, despite how much less convenient they might be in reality. Leaving the apartment in the pitch black and stumbling down the dark hall to the floor's shared bathroom was, of course, *much* more convenient than a gross chamber pot next to the bed. But Tatty was adamant. *We've worked and sacrificed to earn luxuries like running water and flushing toilets. We're going to use them!*

Ester pulled herself to her knees and, using the arm of the couch, climbed over Ruth's sleeping form and tiptoed through the dark apartment to the door. Turning the knob as slowly as she could, she prayed it wouldn't squeak and wake everyone. She stepped out to the hallway and was startled by someone standing there.

"Oh!" Abraham held up his hands. "Sorry, I don't usually see anyone this time of night."

"It's okay." Ester regretted not putting a shawl on over her nightgown. "Wait, are you out here often in the middle of the night?"

Abraham shrugged. "I have trouble sleeping and don't want to keep my father up." He slid down the wall to sit on the floor. Ester crouched down next to him, ignoring her full bladder, and tugged at her nightgown to make sure it covered her legs. She waited to see if he'd say more.

He gave a one-shouldered shrug. "Nightmares, from that day…" he trailed off.

Ester picked at a string on the hem of her nightgown. "I get nightmares often as well."

He shot her a questioning look. "What about?"

She hesitated. The dreams had been weighing on her. Especially with the fresh remnants of one still with her. It would be such a relief to tell someone. He would understand, since he had them himself. "The czar's soldiers. They dragged us all out to the street one day, and tore apart our houses." She wet her lips. "We may not have shared every detail in our letters …"

Abraham gaped, and Ester realized she'd said too much. Ruth and Momme would kill her if they knew. They still didn't want the men to know the full extent of the danger they'd experienced on their own. The guilt was already unbearable.

He finally shook his head and looked away. "Your secret is safe," he said. "But it hurts me that the women see fit to lie to us. Now, I'll wonder what else my family is hiding."

She put a hand on his arm. "I'm sure they're faring better. They're out in the country with your uncle."

He nodded and said nothing.

Ester wracked her brain for some new topic. Why, oh why had she opened her mouth?

"How's school?" he finally asked, his voice gruff.

She flashed him a grateful smile. "Fine, I guess."

"Feeling more comfortable?" he asked in English.

"Some." Ester searched for words in English. "Hedy is helping."

Abraham looked to his hands in his lap. "I'm sorry I haven't helped as much as I told you I would."

Ester chewed her lip. She knew she should tell him it was fine, she understood. But all that came to mind was, she was used to having other members of the family forget their promises—to the point where she almost expected to be shunted aside and neglected. Since they'd come to America, she'd been included only that one day, on the shopping trip. Even a conversation in the kitchen before dinner ended up with her on the outskirts looking in. But it had been that way her entire life. That's what it was like, it seemed, to be the quietest member in a family that was anything but quiet.

Back in Russia, Ruth had been closer to Jeremiah and Abraham—closer in age, closer in friendship. They had done everything together. The formidable trio was known throughout the neighborhood, Ruth happily following along and participating in the rough-and-tumble adventures the boys created. Ester had no interest in climbing trees or kicking balls in the street, but she missed their attention and companionship.

Jeremiah at least made an effort. He'd sneak her candies he'd picked up at the market and sit and tell her *skazkas,* magical tales, of the evil witch, Baba Yaga, or a bird hatched from fire. He taught her to play the piano and how to draw realistic renderings of the birds she loved to watch. It was he who coined her nickname, Little Bird, after stumbling on her crouched in the bush next to their house, spying on the birds in the tree. He joked she'd fallen from her nest as a babe and must really be part bird at heart.

She didn't doubt Ruth loved her. She knew Ruth would do anything for her—she'd guarded Ester like a Mama Bear protecting its cub while they lived in Russia. If anything, that was the problem. Ruth treated her like a child instead of an equal. Ester had hoped and prayed that arriving in New York would change all that. That they could finally be *friends*. Unfortunately, the opposite seemed to be happening. Away from the day-to-day dangers of Russia, the crime and chaos of a desperately poor country on the brink of war, Ruth seemed to almost forget Ester completely. Like she'd released a burden she no longer needed to carry.

Ester took a deep breath and looked up to Abraham. "I'm just glad you and Ruth are together again. It's good to see you two so happy."

Abraham smiled. "*A sheynem dank*. We're feeling our way. Finding our place." He nodded to her. "What about you? You making new friends?"

Ester tilted her head. "A bit. Hedy has introduced me to people."

"Ya? What people?"

Ester picked at the hem of her nightgown again, feeling suddenly shy. "She's been taking me to the settlement house to meet the Educational Alliance people. She's part of a special group working to preserve Jewish culture here in America."

Abraham shifted his weight on the floor to put one knee up. "How so exactly?"

Ester rolled the string on her nightgown between

her fingers. "Well, if you look at many of the Jews who came here before us, the focus was on *becoming* Americans. Which was important. But they, um, lost part of themselves and their culture along the way."

"I can see that. Like my friend, Yankel, no offense to him. But you'd have no clue that he's Jewish. I don't think he's even found a synagogue."

Ester leaned forward. "Exactly. Many of the students at my school are the same way. And worse, most of them are so focused on learning English, they barely speak Yiddish at all anymore."

Abraham scratched his head. "So, what are Hedy and her group proposing to do about it? We can't force people to remain Jewish."

"No, we can't. But we can provide more choices. Hedy believes that most newly arrived Jews are unaware they have another option. Like me, for instance. My teacher told me I needed to improve my English, so I assumed I had to. But why? What need do I have for English in my life besides school?"

Abraham chuckled. "I said the same thing to Ruth about her desire to learn English, but she got insulted."

Ester ignored his comment and plunged ahead. "Hedy says instead of just focusing on Americanization classes, like these cooking and English classes at the settlement house and school, we should be focusing on educating the Jewish children being raised here in America about their roots. Like the yeshiva schools back home."

Abraham raised his eyebrows. "Children, or just the boys?"

Ester smiled. "All Jewish children. Why just the boys when girls will be the mothers raising the children? Shouldn't they know the doctrine and traditions they'll uphold in their homes?"

Abraham nodded "What role do you have in this?"

Ester felt her cheeks grow warm. "Oh, I'm just observing and learning. Hedy and the others have been here longer and are more educated than me."

Abraham smiled. "I think you might be selling yourself short. You have plenty to offer."

She opened her mouth to respond when the door flew open. Samuel stuck his head out, "Would you two lovebirds give it a rest? Some of us—." His voice cut off as he looked down at them. "Oh, Ester, I'm sorry, I assumed…"

She jumped up. "I was going to the bathroom."

She scurried off, leaving the two of them murmuring. She frowned at the guilty flip in her stomach. They were just talking. But she couldn't help her lips curving up into a smile as she remembered his comment about her having plenty to offer.

R u t h

The machines whirled with frantic energy. The holidays loomed closer and orders poured in. Weary from the late nights and early mornings, Ruth asked Chayele if they were given any extra pay for the extra hours. Chayele laughed in response.

A movement caught her eye. It was Grosevich, maneuvering down the aisles with a tray. Ugh, the meat pies again. He came around with them every time he feared their energy might flag. But he demanded praise for doing so. Her tired body tingled with anger as she watched Filomena and Mirele bow their heads to Grosevich and gush about his generosity.

Grosevich took a meat pie and handed it to Ruth.

She looked away and focused on her work.

He sputtered, his cheeks turning bright red. "You ungrateful *Chaya*. Think you're too good to accept the owners' generosity?"

"I'm not hungry." She glared until he moved away.

"What's with you?" Filomena took a bite out of her pie. "I mean they're not great, but it's better than nothing. Aren't you hungry?"

Ruth slammed down her scissors. "You know my feelings on that disgusting man. Besides, the owners keep us these extra hours without pay and we're supposed to gush over a meat pie?" She shook her head and grabbed another blouse with a trembling hand. "It's just not right."

Chayele took the blouse from Ruth. "Don't work when you're angry. You'll just make a mistake and they'll dock your pay."

"No one is saying the pies make up for the unfairness of the situation. Or that we're fans of Grosevich." Zusa wiped her hands on her skirt. "But refusing them hurts no one but you."

Ruth pumped her foot to power up her machine again. "I guess the stress is getting to me."

"Oh, trust me, we feel it too." Mirele cracked her knuckles. "I've lost three dollars in the last three weeks, courtesy of Mr. Blanck and Mr. Harris."

Zusa chuckled. "Three? I'm up to four. I had to turn down another load last night."

Ruth stopped her machine and stared at the girls. "What do you mean you're losing money?"

Chayele patted Ruth's hand. "They take in extra laundry and sewing for neighbors to help cover their expenses. As do many of the girls in the factory without families."

"And by being forced to stay longer, you can't complete your work at home." Ruth shook her head.

Mirele shrugged. "We'll survive. We always do."

They fell into silence for the next few hours. The drone of the machines was interspersed only by the crack of a knuckle or neck. Ruth's eyelids grew heavier and harder to keep open as the evening wore on. Thankfully, it was Saturday and they would finally get a break tomorrow. As the last hour wound down, Ruth was startled out of her grogginess by shouts from the cutting tables.

"You lying *gonif*!"

One of the cutters leapt over the table and lunged at Grosevich. The other cutters grabbed for his arms and pulled him back.

Grosevich folded his arms and glared at the man. "Pull yourself together! Mistakes always equal less pay. This is not news."

"You lie! There were no mistakes!" The cutter lunged again, waving his pay envelope. "This *dreck* barely covers what you owe me, let alone all my men."

Ruth recognized the man as one of the more respected contractors who'd been working in the factory for years. His team of men relied on him to negotiate on their behalf. She looked around and saw that all work had ceased and everyone was staring at the unfolding disturbance, waiting to see what would happen next.

Grosevich gestured to security. Two large security guards grabbed the contractor and dragged him to the door. His feet squeaked on the floor as he struggled. "Don't just sit there—they're crooks—stop letting them—"

Grosevich turned back to the rest of the floor. He waved his arms and thundered over the contractor's pleas. "What are you waiting for? Get back to work!"

Ruth's fists balled up in her lap. Across the room,

she saw Abraham move away from his table and step closer to the fray. His shoulders were tense and his mouth a hard line. No one spoke as the contractor was finally pulled out the door and away. Finally, there was stunned silence.

The sound of scraping chairs pierced the tense air.

"Enough!" one girl shouted.

"Stop the injustice!" said another.

One by one, girls stood across the factory floor. Two cutters swept fabric from their tables to the floor and exited where the contractor had been recently dragged. The other standing girls followed.

"If you leave, you will be fired!" Grosevich climbed to a tabletop and stomped his foot to get attention. "If you walk out that door, there's no coming back, I'm warning you."

His cracking voice was soon overpowered by a chant reverberating off the factory walls.

"Strike! Stop the injustice!"

Workers pushed past the table where Grosevich was standing and flowed to the staircase door.

Ruth's head was whirling and she could hardly catch her breath. Her body, recently so limp and exhausted, was now buzzing with excitement. Could she do this? Could she join this walk-out? She'd lose her job if she did. She tried to catch Abraham's eye, but he turned away. She stood, but lost sight of him in the surge of people.

Chayele leapt to her feet, overturning her chair in the process. "Now's our chance, Ruth." She grabbed Ruth's arm and pulled her away from the table. "Enough talk, time for action."

Chayele kept hold of Ruth's right arm and Zusa took hold of her left. Ruth looked over her shoulder and saw Filomena and Mirele following. But, she could see not everyone had gotten up from their seats. A few remained, looking terrified. One girl clutched the table like it would save her from drowning.

Ruth's stomach swirled. Was she really doing this? Images of Grosevich refusing her pay and him leaning over the terrified girl flashed through her head. Yes, it was time for action.

Ruth turned back to Chayele, and together she and her friends walked down the narrow aisle between the machines to join the chanting crowd making its way down the staircase.

✳ ✳ ✳

"What do you mean you walked out?" Tatty roared. "What were you thinking?"

"And where's Abraham?" Momme asked.

Side by side, they glared across the kitchen table at Ruth. Ester and Samuel hovered by the door.

Ruth waved Momme off. "We got separated in the chaos. I walked home with the girls. You'd understand if you were there. Everyone came together."

The front door opened and Abraham entered. Before he could slide his coat off, Tatty turned on him.

"And what about you? Did you also join in this *fercokt* uprising?"

Abraham removed his coat and hung it.

"No, I stayed and completed my shift."

Tatty smiled. He turned to Ruth. "At least your boy has sense."

Ignoring Tatty, Ruth rose from her chair and grabbed Abraham by the arm. "You stayed? You finished your shift?"

"Tatty, come." Momme pulled Tatty gently. He tore his hand away from her and shook his head.

Momme glared at him before going into the bedroom by herself.

Abraham swallowed hard, glancing first at Tatty and then Ruth. "I've been on the front lines of an uprising before, Ruth. I've seen the cost of such actions. I don't expect you to understand."

"But you saw that man get cheated today. You saw *me* get cheated! And that little girl, attacked by Grosevich—she was no older than Ester!"

He reached for her, but she stepped away.

"No, Abraham. I don't understand. How can you condone this when everyone around you is speaking out? It almost seems—"

She stopped, a sudden lump in her throat. "Are you... Are you that much of a coward?"

Tatty slammed his fist on the kitchen table. "Don't you ever call him that!"

Abraham turned to Tatty and sighed. "She wasn't there, Jacob. Leave her be."

She wasn't there. She realized he wasn't talking about today. He was talking about the protests in Russia—the protests in which Jeremiah died.

Tatty glared at Ruth over the table before turning away and slamming into his bedroom.

Ruth and Abraham stood in awkward silence in the kitchen. She heard Samuel's voice faintly from the parlor, where he'd begun reading Scripture to Ester.

Abraham rubbed his finger over the top of the kitchen chair, avoiding her eyes.

Ruth cleared her throat. "Is this about Russia? About Bloody Sunday?"

His head shot up. Pain glimmered in his eyes.

She took a small step to him. "Help me understand, Abraham. Tell me what happened. I've never heard the story."

He leaned forward, gripping the chair for support.

"The images are forever burned in my brain." His breath hissed out. "Not a day goes by where I don't wish we stayed home playing cards with you, instead of going on that march."

"But you were trying to get help from the czar to end the strike, ya?" She put a hand on his back.

"It was Mark's idea to trust Father Gapon and join his peaceful march to Winter Palace to present our complaints to the czar. They swore there would be no violence. And there wasn't—on *our* part."

"We heard the soldiers opened fire on the crowd…" Ruth urged him on.

Abraham nodded. When he spoke, his voice was choked. "Ya. They were first aiming for Father Gapon, I think. But Mark went down first. Then the Father. But they kept firing! The bullets just kept coming." He shook his head and gulped the air before continuing. "Jeremiah was standing next to Mark, just trying to help him. When Jeremiah was shot, he fell right by my feet. The blood…Someone jostled me and I almost stepped on him, Ruth."

He went silent and his shoulders shook.

Ruth rested her head on his chest and patted his back. "Shh. There was nothing you could do."

They stood embracing for a few minutes while he cried softly. Finally, he sniffled and stepped away from her, wiping his eyes.

"I won't do it again, Ruth. We stood up against injustice then, and for what? What did we gain? I watched my brother and best friend die at my feet, and yet the injustice went on."

Ruth was about to respond when a knock at the door interrupted. She moved away to answer.

Chayele and Yankel stood in the hallway.

"What are you two doing out this late?" Ruth motioned them in.

Yankel shook his head as they shuffled in. "Leave it to my sister to immediately charge ahead. I'm just following along, chaperoning."

Chayele hit him on the arm. "This is too important to wait. We're spreading the word that in light of what occurred today, the Garment Workers' Union has called an emergency meeting tomorrow at eleven."

"We'll be there."

Chayele smiled and squeezed Ruth's hand. "Isn't

this better than refusing the meat pies?"

Ruth laughed and showed them back out. She closed the door and took a deep breath before turning back to face Abraham.

He crossed his arms. "*We'll* be there? I didn't realize I'd agreed to join the cause."

"But Abraham, don't you see? We could work together to finish the fight. It might not be Russia, but it's the same enemy. The factories are forcing us down here, too. Cheating us, overworking us. All so the rich can prosper off our suffering. It needs to end. Don't let Jeremiah and Mark's deaths be for nothing."

He shook his head and used two fingers to squeeze the bridge of his nose. "It's not that simple! People like Max Blanck and Isaac Harris are not just going to roll over and give in."

She put her hand on his arm.

"Then we fight. Mark and Jeremiah did. They wouldn't want you backing down now. There are many battles to win the war, right?"

She stepped closer again, and he opened his arms and took her in. As she laid her head on his chest, she felt him nod. A rush of emotion flooded through her. They were in this together. She pulled him closer. Their love was so new. She wanted to protect it, let it grow strong. But she also wanted to do what was right. She felt him cling to her. She breathed in the smell of him and closed her eyes.

* * *

As Abraham and Ruth opened the door to the union hall the following day, a wave of heat crashed over them. A crowd of people stood shoulder to shoulder across the back of the room. Rows of chairs faced a makeshift stage with two aisles for traffic between. Seated in the chairs, girls chattered, turning to face each other.

"Ruth! Abraham! Over here!" Chayele waved from the other side of the hall.

Ruth took Abraham's hand and pushed through the crowd to where the girls stood with Yankel. Abraham pulled back and motioned to the back wall by the door. She shook her head. He shrugged and let go of her hand.

She searched his face. "You're not staying?"

"I just want to stay by the door."

"Are you sure?" She felt torn. She took in his slumped shoulders and the bags beneath his eyes. She glanced at her happy friends.

"Go," he said, waving her off. "I'm fine."

She gave him a quick peck on the cheek and made her way to join her friends. Chayele pulled Ruth into their circle. They greeted her with sparkling eyes and warm hugs. Ruth, caught up in their giddy excitement, forgot about Abraham for a moment. When she did take a breath and glance over her shoulder, she found him listlessly staring at the floor. A tingling of concern flashed through her, but Mirele and Zusa started talking to her and she turned away.

"Can you believe this turnout?" Zusa asked.

"How'd you get the word out?" Mirele asked.

Chayele smiled. "The union had volunteers spread out and contact people from other garment shops across town. Then the gossip mills did the rest. News of a walk-out in the biggest garment factory in the city traveled fast."

"Do you think they'll agree to strike?" Ruth asked.

Mirele shrugged. "We're hoping so, but no one knows the union leaders' intentions yet. They were hesitant to act for the strikes with the smaller factories in the past. But maybe now with the size and reputation of the Triangle?"

Zusa shushed them and pointed as three of the leaders made their way up the steps to the stage. One of the men stepped to the podium. He waited until the chatter died down. Then he and the two other men addressed the crowd for the next forty-five minutes.

"Are they making sense?" Filomena whispered.

"Not really. They're saying something about negotiation with the owners and the need for solidarity." Zusa shrugged. "But they're just repeating themselves as far as I can tell."

"I didn't know if it was perhaps the language," Filomena said.

"No, they're just trying to confuse us so we can't tell they're avoiding the subject of a strike." Chayele twirled a lock of hair. "Cowards."

"Is anything going to come from this, or did we just lose our jobs for nothing?" Mirele whimpered.

Ruth squeezed her hand. "Don't lose faith. Look at all the people here. We're not the only ones looking for change."

Suddenly, there was a disturbance on the floor. People began whispering and pointing as a tall woman emerged from a row of chairs. The woman pulled herself up to her full height and lifted her hands to straighten her hat. She walked determinedly up to the stage. The whispers grew louder as she climbed the steps and walked directly to the podium.

"Excuse me, please." She gestured for the man to move aside. "I'm Clara Lemlich and I'd like to say a few words."

The man at the podium looked over his shoulder at the other men behind him for direction. One of them shrugged and the man took a begrudging step back.

She immediately slammed her fist on the podium. "Enough of this *hok a chainik*. Let's get to the point. Do we want to strike?"

From all corners of the room girls stood, shouting a resounding "Yes!"

Clara smiled. "There's power in numbers."

"If you are with me, you will join me in taking this oath of loyalty." Clara raised her right hand and waited for the rest of the room to follow. She then began saying in Yiddish, "If I turn traitor to the cause I now pledge, may this hand wither from the arm I raise."

Ruth felt chills run down her spine as everyone in the room repeated the oath in unison. Change was about to happen. She felt it.

Clara stepped away from the podium. She turned back to the union leaders who stood with their arms crossed, glaring at her.

"Thank you, gentlemen," she said, bowing her head to them. "I'll leave you to inform the factories the garment workers are on strike."

The room erupted with cheers. Ruth and the girls bounced on their toes, hugging in excitement. As she embraced Filomena, Ruth looked past her shoulder to Abraham, still leaning against the wall with a strained expression on his face. She broke away from Filomena and ran to him.

She patted his arm. "It'll be okay. Power in numbers, right?"

He shrugged off her hand. "We'll see how your numbers are after a few days on the picket line."

"Must you be so pessimistic?" She turned her back to him and looked over the cheering crowd. The girls' faces were flushed and grinning. They crowded around Clara Lemlich, shouting questions. She was young—no older than Ruth and her friends. And yet this woman had taken charge of the room with confidence and strength. Yes, this time would be different. They would *make* the factory owners listen. This was America after all, not Russia. Here, change happened all the time.

A b r a h a m

Sunday November 22nd, 1909

487 Days Until the Fire

It was happening again. He remained silent as they walked home while Ruth spoke excitedly with her friends. She didn't seem to notice his silence. If anything, she was probably chalking it up to him still being "grumpy." But what Abraham felt was more like terrified. Ruth still failed to fully grasp that he'd lived this before. He'd been in her place—full of faith and open to risk for revolutionary change.

It had been a freezing cold night in January. Abraham felt the wind whip through his coat deep into his bones as they left the Assembly Meeting.

"Didn't I tell you he was amazing?" Mark asked, waving to some other men leaving the building.

Mark put an arm around Abraham and Jeremiah and gave them a quick squeeze as they set off to home. "I'm telling you boys, Father Gapon, he's the key. If we follow him, the czar will listen. The czar will make the factory concede."

"Why would a priest lead an underground Assembly of Russian Workers?" Jeremiah asked as he rubbed his hands together to warm them.

Mark laughed. "Oh, he's no ordinary priest, as you could see. Gapon's got a history. He's seen a lot. Grew up with hardship. He sees what the factories do to us. How they turn their backs when you're hurt and no longer of use to them."

Abraham opened his mouth to respond when Mark shushed him. He nodded his head to the sky and Abraham took note of the watch-tower looming overhead as they passed. A police officer's formidable form was standing guard. Watching all.

They tipped their hats to the officer and shuffled past, holding their breath. Abraham waited for the officer to call out. To somehow know where they were coming from, what they were plotting.

Despite Mark's reassurances, could they be viewed as a threat to the czar? Was he crazy to go along with this march?

He thought of his fellow workers, some of whom had been recently fired for their suspected "treasonous associations" with the Assembly. The entire factory had walked out in a supportive strike. But here they were, three weeks later, and the factory still showed no sign of rehiring the fired workers. It was almost Christmas and bitterly cold, and Abraham's family had barely enough wood left for the stove. They were hitting the end of their savings, and he knew they weren't the only ones.

Father Gapon's plan was a desperate, grasping reach, but surely it wasn't unreasonable. A petition to the czar would be viewed as a respectful act, not treason. After all, the workers weren't revolutionaries! They weren't Bolsheviks trying to upend the customs and institutions of Russia. They just wanted a job with fair wages, decent hours, and protection from harm. But would the czar listen? Would he agree to intervene?

Father Gapon believed he would. So much so,

he'd made a grand speech rallying them all to join him. "This must be a noble endeavor. There can be no political demands. Tear up your leaflets supporting revolutionary aims! The czar is appointed by God. As long as he is made aware of our circumstances, we must trust he will do right by us."

Jeremiah cleared his throat. "Do we actually believe him? Or should I say, do we believe he's right about the czar?"

Mark shrugged. "What's the alternative? And after all, the czar has intervened for protesting workers before."

"He hasn't been so fair to the Jews," put in Jeremiah.

"We have to have faith," said Mark, simply.

Abraham said nothing, just gazed at the city through the cold cloud of his breath. He loved this city. His home. The shadowy domes of St. Alexander's and St. Isaac's cathedrals towering over the darkened city. He wanted more than anything to put aside his doubts and listen to Mark and Father Gapon and trust in the czar to protect them.

He looked to his older brother's raised eyebrows

and sighed. "Okay, I'm in. Jeremiah?"

Jeremiah nodded. "Me too. What's the worst that can happen?"

Mark whooped and swung his arms around their shoulders again. "That's the spirit! Just think, we can always look back and say we took a chance, right? We were there, making history."

Abraham and Jeremiah glanced at each other before nodding. Mark grinned at them and they walked home, pushing and pestering each other as only young men can.

"What's the worst that can happen?" Abraham pinched the bridge of his nose and groaned. He still couldn't believe Jeremiah had actually asked that. If only he could go back and answer him. *You'll get gunned down while singing "God Save the Czar" as you march peacefully to Winter Palace.* But no, they'd decided to trust and have faith in the system. In the good of their leader.

Now he was watching Ruth do the same with this Clara Lemlich woman—another charismatic speaker who was swaying the crowd to take a gigantic risk with little guarantee of reward. Did they honestly think the Triangle Shirtwaist Kings were going to cave? That a bunch of foreigners from the tenements would upend the garment industry?

He tensed as a heavy hand clapped his shoulder.

Yankel laughed. "Why are you a grumpy goat?"

Abraham took a deep breath. Yankel's gesture was so familiar that for a moment he'd actually imagined he'd turn to see Jeremiah or Mark there.

"Not grumpy. Just skeptical. What are your honest thoughts on this? Are you buying this 'strike and change will happen' idea?"

Yankel rubbed the stubble on his chin. "I don't know. Maybe?" He shrugged. "Look, I get you've done this and know more than the rest of us. But it's not that simple."

He gestured to Ruth and the girls up ahead. "Right now, your wonderful fiancée believes in hope and good in the world. She had a hard time in Russia from what I can gather, but, well, she still has that idealism. Do you really want to deprive her of that?"

Abraham looked where Yankel pointed. Ruth was laughing and talking animatedly with her friends. She looked carefree and happy.

Yankel adjusted his hat. "Think of cutting yourself a break too, Abe. I know you don't like to talk about what happened, and there's more you're not telling me. But, do you really want to go through life believing the worst will always happen?"

He winked and turned to the girls. "Chayele! It's late." He jerked his thumb to their block.

Chayele began her goodbyes, promising to talk more in the morning. The group disbanded with everyone going off in different directions.

Abraham gave Ruth his arm as they turned homeward. She gave him a dazzling smile that nearly took his breath away.

No, he couldn't deprive her of her view of the world. He just hoped no one else would either.

R u t h

"Where is she?" Mirele asked. "Clara's never been late before."

"You don't think she's giving up?" Zusa asked.

Ruth looked at the many empty seats in the hall, evidence of their dwindling forces. A month and a half had passed since Clara first stood in front of the assembled garment workers, and many had lost hope. Even Abraham had escorted her to the meeting and opted to go have a pint with Yankel rather than stay for the discussion. Morale was down.

Smaller factories had offered to settle—those that couldn't survive a drawn-out battle or afford to hire scabs at double the price. They needed their workforce and agreed to demands so they'd return.

But the behemoth Triangle still showed no interest in negotiating. They had full pocketbooks and could always find other workers to fill the lines. The only way to get results was through solidarity. The workers hoped to reignite that solidarity tonight. Reinforce the idea that *all* workers' needs should be met. They needed all the factories to remain closed. If so, the Triangle would be pressured to negotiate.

The meeting had been Clara's idea. Although she didn't work at the Triangle herself, she viewed things in big picture. She'd become the uprising's unofficial leader—creating makeshift podiums wherever she was, preaching about the need for sweeping change across the entire garment industry.

They'd all gotten to know Clara over the last few weeks. Chayele in particular, viewed Clara as a mentor of sorts. She followed Clara everywhere, even emulating her style and mannerisms. Ruth understood Chayele's fascination. If Ruth had more freedom herself, she'd cozy up to Clara as well. Unfortunately, Abraham couldn't stand Clara. He viewed her as a dangerous instigator.

Ruth and her friends spoke of Clara often, analyzing her words and ideas. She made it sound possible to achieve long-lasting results from the strike. As long as they stuck together.

But she was now almost half an hour late.

Ruth turned to Chayele. "You spoke with her last. Did she show any sign of backing out?"

"Never," Chayele said emphatically. "She's always remained firm on the power in numbers. She wouldn't abandon us."

Ruth chewed her lip. She glanced at the three union leaders gathered at the table in front. She'd long ago dubbed them Mustache Fellow, Lemon Face and Skinny Beanpole to keep them straight. Mustache Fellow was glancing at his pocket watch and gesturing to the others. What if they left? They'd already been losing patience with the ongoing strike and the resentment of the factory owners. It was costing the union a fortune to continue bailing the girls out of jail from arrests made on the picket lines.

Chairs squeaked as the men stood to gather their things. Ruth looked to the door. Where was Clara?

"Wait!" Chayele leapt to her feet. "We can still present our argument. Right, girls?"

Zusa, Mirele and Filomena stood. Ruth reluctantly joined them. She couldn't speak to an entire room full of people! How could *they* convince the union leaders? But then, Clara was only a nineteen-year-old girl as well. How was she any different?

Ruth looked to her friends. Chayele stood with a lifted chin. Where did she get this confidence?

Skinny Beanpole whispered something to the other leaders. After a brief discussion, they sat back down. Chayele cleared her throat.

"Gentlemen," she said, her voice shaking a bit.

The door crashed open and Clara slumped in. Her face was bloody and bruised.

"Oh, my goodness! What happened?" Filomena rushed to Clara's side. Others followed, surrounding Clara in a group.

"Is she okay? Should I get ice?" Zusa asked.

"No, a warm compress," Mirele said.

Other girls piped in with other remedy ideas.

Clara shoved through them and pushed her way to the front of the room. The girls fell back in consternation. Skinny Beanpole rushed to get her a chair. He then offered her a handkerchief which she accepted and held to her head.

After she was settled with the reddening

handkerchief at her head, and a glass of water, she finally spoke.

"It was the Triangle's owner, Max Blanck—his thugs giving me a warning!"

The union leaders exchanged a look. Mustache Fellow cleared his throat. "Do you have any proof your attackers have a connection to him?"

Chayele threw her hands in the air. "What proof do you need? Look at her! Who else would it be?"

Ruth looked at her hands as other girls chimed in. Max Blanck couldn't be that evil? Could he?

Hiring thugs to beat up a woman!

Lemon Face stood and gestured for quiet. As usual he had his trademark sour expression. "I don't disagree that it looks suspicious. But what my colleague meant was, we have no actual evidence tying Mr. Blanck to the attack."

The door opened again and two police officers strode into the room. They were immediately met with boos and name-calling.

Mustache Fellow rushed to meet them. "We know she needs to give a statement," Mustache Fellow said. "But can it wait, please?" He gestured to the door, trying to get the officers to wait outside.

The two officers exchanged a look and instead

stood in the back of the room with their arms crossed.

Clara struggled to her feet and shuffled forward. She stood waiting until the room fell silent. "We've lost sight of why we're here today. If anything, allow my current condition to be a reminder why we need to remain united. We can't return to work until all the factories have conceded!"

She sat down heavily as the room erupted again.

Ruth stared at Clara's bruised face. She still had some gravel clinging to a cut on her forehead. Ruth's thoughts churned. How had things gotten so out of control? How did Clara garner this strength? Who was this woman? Had she been a girl just like Ruth, going to and from work each day before the strike?

The union leaders calmed the room and demanded that people take turns to express their views. "We'll declare a vote at the end," Mustache Fellow shouted.

A red-haired Irish girl stood to speak, her musical brogue softening her words. "I'm sorry for you all. But my mother's ill! When I was offered my job back, I had to take it."

A small, dark Italian girl spoke over her. "Look what they've done to Clara. Can't you see—our only chance is to stick together!"

A man stood. "I agree. What about a settlement for all? And power in numbers?"

The Irish girl made to respond, but another girl interrupted. "If your mother's ill, ask friends, ask neighbors for help. We must care for one another."

Everyone was on their feet now, shouting over each other. A tall girl cried in Yiddish, "It's the Triangle's fault! You started this mess!"

People around her nodded in agreement.

"You walked off."

"Now you want us to support you."

"We've done our part!"

Shouts of "Hear, hear!" came from around the room. Ruth turned to Zusa and Mirele sitting next to her. Filomena sat at the end of the row with clacking knitting needles to keep her nervous hands busy.

"What are we going to do?" Ruth cried. "They're turning on us."

Mirele shook her head. "They're desperate."

"It's survival," Zusa agreed. "It's hard to think of others when your stomach is empty."

"Wait—are you saying you agree?" Ruth asked.

"I understand. I didn't say I agreed," Mirele said.

Zusa chewed her lip. "I'd be hard-pressed to say what I would do if my mother were sick."

Ruth watched as the crowd continued to argue. The union leaders sat at the table, heads together, scribbling notes as the girls spoke. Finally, Lemon Face stood. "I think we've heard enough. Let's take a brief break and then we'll proceed with a vote."

Ruth and her friends gathered by the vacant table at the front of the room with Chayele and Clara. The union leaders had fled the room immediately to avoid being waylaid with pleas.

"This wait might be worse than the strike itself," Clara joked.

Chayele chuckled nervously and nibbled on a fingernail. Ruth noticed that the rest of her fingernails looked like bloody stumps. The stress was getting to them all. Zusa's lip was chapped and bruised from her own chewing and Mirele was going to have a bald spot soon from her constant hair twirling. The only one who had anything positive to show for her nervous energy was Filomena. She had finished half a scarf.

The door opened and the union leaders returned. Everyone scurried back to their seats.

Skinny Beanpole stood in front of the others. "To make this as quick and painless as possible, we will proceed immediately with a vote. We'll go for a simple 'aye' and 'nay' and raising of hands to pass the motion. Agreed?"

The girls nodded. Zusa grabbed Ruth's arm.

"All those in favor of continuing to support the Triangle workers in a universal strike?"

"Aye!" Chayele and Clara shouted from the front.

"Aye!" Ruth and her friends called out as well. Around the room, other girls continued to raise their hands and cast their vote. Ruth frantically turned in her seat, attempting to count hands. It would be close. Too close. Mustache Fellow and Lemon Face walked around counting hands and marking a tally on pieces of paper. They nodded to Skinny Beanpole in front.

"All opposed?"

Cries of "nay" sounded from throughout the room. The Irish girl raised her hand high, as did many of the workers from factories who had settled.

Zusa squeezed Ruth's arm harder, to the point of pain. Ruth's chest constricted at the sight of all the raised hands. The leaders returned to the front and checked their tallies at the table.

Skinny Beanpole cleared his throat. "The votes have been counted. The universal strike is over. Settled factories will return to work and Triangle workers will be left to strike on their own. We'll continue to negotiate on their behalf."

The room erupted in chaos. Clara slumped in her chair and cried. Chayele reached over to hold her hand. Filomena's needles clacked even more furiously, as if she could knit away reality.

Ruth turned to Zusa and Mirele. She opened her mouth to speak, but realized she had nothing to say. They appeared to have nothing either. The three of them leaned forward and held hands in silence as the noise of the room swirled around them.

Ester

Monday January 15th, 1910

432 Days Until the Fire

Ester yawned as she wrung out the water from yet another shirt. Her hands were already stinging and turning red. Monday laundry days were the worst. At least the apartment had running water, so they didn't have to tote up heavy pots from the backyard pump like some of her classmates in other buildings.

Ester passed the newly cleaned shirt to Momme, who clipped it onto the clothes line. Momme wheeled the now-full line out into the space between buildings and waved to a neighbor doing the same across the way. Ester wondered when it had become general practice for everyone to do their laundry on Mondays. The entire courtyard was filled with flapping garments.

She picked up another shirt and rubbed her forehead with her arm before she plunged the shirt into the soapy water. Momme turned from the window and shivered. "It's going to freeze. I wish we had basement lines like some of those buildings on Delancey."

Ester shrugged. "But then we'd have to carry it all up and down the stairs."

Momme sighed and turned back to the window, staring at nothing. Ester continued scrubbing the shirt. She wondered what Momme was thinking about—if she was happy here in New York. She knew Momme was glad to be reunited with Tatty and away from the violence and poverty of St. Petersburg. But what of the friends they'd left behind in the *shtetl*? Momme had yet to make any new friends here, and she resisted the *Shabbat* ladies who reached out.

Ester assumed it was pride—she was ashamed to be viewed as the charity case, needing food sent on Fridays. The food was helpful with Ruth and Abraham out of work, but each time it arrived, Momme got very quiet, her lips in a straight line.

She'd say thank you and remind them she was perfectly capable of providing a *Shabbat* meal for her family herself.

She'd barely even explored the bustling Orchard Street marketplace that captured her attention when they'd first arrived. Instead, as soon as breakfast was done each day, she'd write up a list for dinner that night and ask Ester to pick up the ingredients on her way home from school. Come to think of it, Momme rarely left the apartment at all.

Ester cleared her throat as she wrung the shirt in her hands. "So, Hedy and I had a confusing conversation last night."

Momme turned to her. "Oh? What about?"

"They've opened a new training college for Jewish teachers. They want to open a set of Jewish schools in the city." Ester looked down at the soapy water and her hair fell in front of her face.

Momme harrumphed. "What, so more boys and men can while away the day studying Scripture?"

"Actually, they plan to focus on cultivating female teachers to teach all Jewish children." Ester handed another shirt to Momme. "Hedy thinks I should apply. Crazy, right?"

"Interesting." Momme clipped the shirt to the

clothing line. "Did I ever tell you that you remind me of my mother? She loved all the rituals to her bones. The Jewish practices were everything to her. To some extent, she would probably disapprove of what this Hedy is doing. Can you compromise on the accepted roles of life and household? Of course, she never saw America—she would probably be horrified by a lot of what goes on here."

Momme smiled. "She cooked and stored food weeks before holidays— then opened the doors to everyone in the village!"

Ester picked up a pair of pants and dunked them in the water, giving her mother space to continue.

Momme wrapped her arms around herself. "I'll never forget the day we lost it all. All that joy and love, gone in a flash. I was playing outside with girls I'd known my whole life, girls who'd come with their families to eat at our table. Suddenly, mothers swooped in grabbing their daughters away, as if my presence would harm them. The *pogroms* began that night. Mobs of outsiders joined by our own neighbors sweeping through, ripping Jews from their homes.

"I hid under the bed in my parents' room while my parents whispered about the absurdity of these rumors. Jews responsible for the czar's murder? My father kept repeating that people would come to their senses and this would all pass."

Momme turned back to Ester and swallowed. Tears glistened in her eyes. "We all survived that night, but they came for my father the next night. I never saw him again."

Ester froze while the pants dripped through her fingers. She'd never heard this story before. She'd known Momme had survived pogroms, that people from her village had turned on Jews and had them transported to the *Pale*—a settlement for Jews in exile. It's why Momme had ended up in St. Petersburg, escaping the vindictiveness and suspicion of village life. But she'd never heard what happened to her grandparents. She'd just always assumed they'd died.

Ester inhaled. "What happened to your mother?"

Momme looked at the floor. "She was sent to the *Pale*. As far as I know, she's still there. We write letters now and then."

Her grandmother was still alive? Thoughts moved through Ester's mind, pieces of stories and history clicking and falling into place. She suddenly understood better her mother's tendency to avoid neighbors, to only cultivate a few trusted friendships.

But why was Momme telling her this now? Ester wrung out the dripping pants and thought carefully about how to phrase her next question.

"Momme, why do you still fight so hard to be a Jew then? I mean, if it's caused so much suffering…"

Momme tilted her head and thought a moment. "It keeps me attached to my roots. My parents. Being Jewish is more than just practicing a religion. It's my heritage, my history. We're part of a lineage going back for generations, along with the traditions and practices we pass down."

Momme reached for the pair of pants Ester held and clipped them to the clothes line. "What about you? Why do you think Hedy suggested you apply?"

Ester glanced at the basket next to the tub and inwardly groaned when she saw only the bed linens remaining. They were the most difficult to manage. "My feelings are similar. But I'm afraid those practices might die out or become something we no longer recognize if we don't intervene."

Momme grabbed the other side of the sheet Ester was dunking and scrubbed. "How so?"

Ester gestured with a soapy hand. "Because it's already happening. There's already this divide in our community. Look at these girls Ruth's met at the factory—would you even know they're Jewish? They skip synagogue, they speak less Yiddish and more English. They call it assimilating, but what will remain to pass on to the next generation?"

She reached back into the tub to finish scrubbing her side. "And then there are the Jews turning inwards, who refuse to speak English, who only interact with other Jews. It's almost like they're recreating their *shtetls* here, refusing to assimilate at all."

Momme wrung the sheet, pulling so sharply she ripped it from Ester's fingers. "You have a problem with this?"

Ester wrapped her fingers around the edge of the tub and took a deep breath. "I fear they're missing out. Why can't we have both? Retain our heritage and embrace America, too? That's what these new schools want to do. To help us have *both.*"

Momme pinned the sheet to the line. "This is something you want, this combining of worlds?"

Ester put her hand on top of Momme's on the sheet. "Isn't that why we came? To practice our faith without fear? To work hard and reap the benefits of success without worrying they'll be taken from us?" Ester nodded to Momme's stomach, to what she knew Momme was hiding. "For the next generation to grow knowing they can be whatever they want?"

Momme put a hand over her stomach. "So you know, huh?"

Ester nodded. "But I haven't said anything."

Momme squeezed Ester's hand. "I'm proud of you. You're so good. They're lucky to have you."

"So, you think I should do it? Apply?"

Momme smiled. "I think you should do whatever you want to do, be whatever you want in this crazy American world."

Ester laughed. "As long as I'm still Jewish?"

"As long as you're still Jewish."

Momme put her arm around Ester's shoulder and the two returned to the washtub to finish the rest of the linens. But Ester felt a new energy buzzing within her. She had a glimmer of what her future could be. She could have a purpose. She could find balance.

R u t h

Wednesday January 19th, 1910

428 Days Until the Fire

A gust of wind swirled through the picket line, allowing the bitter cold to cut to the bone. Ruth inhaled deeply and reminded herself why this was important. They had a purpose, a goal. A reason to be standing here. A little wind could not drive them away.

She shifted the heavy sign from one side to the other and raised it over her head again. Stepping into an icy puddle, she winced as water soaked right through the cardboard Momme had given her to patch the hole in the toe of her right shoe.

She pulled her hat down farther over her ears. It was the last of the good hats her family owned. Shared with Momme and Ester, it was purple wool with pretty green and yellow flowers tucked in the brim. They'd been letting Ruth take it each day she was on the picket line to keep her ears warm.

Abraham came up from behind her and wrapped an arm around her shoulders. "You all right?"

She tried to smile. "Just that hole in my shoe."

At that moment a fancy black car with silver trim and curtained windows turned the corner, driving toward the picket line. It sparkled in the winter sun.

Chayele, standing next to them, snorted. "Figures. Max Blanck refuses to part with a few extra dollars while we're starving, but he can buy himself one of those fancy new limousines."

The car pulled to a stop in front of them. The crowd on the picket line started yelling. Police ran to the car to offer protection. Abraham shifted his grip from Ruth's shoulders to her hand and squeezed. Ruth squeezed back as Blanck, dressed in a tailored suit with a thick, luxurious wool coat and hat, stepped out of the back of the car.

Blanck looked over their way. She felt his disdain. There was no remorse or guilt for leaving them standing out in the cold day after day. He was not going to waver.

Her stomach growled, reminding her of her watered-down oatmeal this morning. This was after their pitiful family dinner last night. Four potatoes shared amongst the six of them. Tatty and Samuel had been working extra hours to make enough money to pay the rent. Ester and Momme had taken in extra sewing, but still, they struggled to survive. It reminded Ruth of the bad times in Russia. She thought she'd escaped constant hunger. She clenched her jaw—all they were asking for were fair working conditions and steady pay that reflected their work. Other factories in the city settled weeks ago! But the Triangle owners were stubbornly holding out.

Ruth knew the strike was even harder on Mirele and Zusa. Eight weeks on the picket line had emptied their meager savings, and they'd been forced to leave their apartment and move in with other girls from the factory. There were now ten of them living together, working through the night sewing for neighbors. Each day the circles under their eyes looked darker.

Abraham pulled her closer to him as some of the workers started throwing rotten food at Blanck and the police officers. Blanck was almost to the door. He turned back to look once more at the ensuing chaos and Ruth could see a sly grin broadening on his face before he ducked inside.

As soon as he disappeared, the police descended upon the crowd. They kicked the barriers aside, fists and batons flying. They met the workers' shouts with punches and slaps. Caught up in the movement, Ruth lost her hold on Abraham's hand.

"Ruth! *Gay Avek*! Run!" he yelled.

Pushing against the momentum of surging people, she glanced down at the ground and saw that the cold, dirty snow now glistened with drops of shiny red blood. All around her, police officers and workers argued and fought. Her stomach heaved as she saw some of the girls' beaten and bloody faces. She faintly heard Chayele and Filomena calling her name, but she couldn't find them.

As the thickest wave of people passed her by, she noticed her pretty purple hat trampled and muddy on the ground. The little yellow flower had broken off. Someone must have knocked it off in the turmoil. They needed that warm hat, even in its current bedraggled state. She and Abraham were already responsible for their growling stomachs each night. She could not return home without a hat to keep

Momme and Ester's heads warm. As she lunged to pick it up, she felt a harsh blow to the back of her head. A flash of pain blinded her.

* * *

"I don't care about your principles!" Tatty yelled. "You will go back to work. No more picket line!"

"Tatty, calm down. I'm fine. Barely a bump." Ruth reached for his hand across the table.

He shook her off and jumped up, the force of his movement sending his chair falling backwards.

"Barely a bump? You're all *furshlugginer* and bandaged." He gestured at her head.

"Yes, but there were witnesses who saw the police beating us," she said.

"After your *fercockt* crowd threw rotten fruit at the man! You're no better than he is!" He waved his finger at her. "No more consorting with these *chayas*!"

"I can't, Tatty. We've come too far. The strike *will* work. But only if we stick together!"

Tatty threw his arms up into the air. "What? You're willing to sacrifice yourself and your family?"

Locking gazes with her father, she sat back in her chair and folded her arms.

"We made a vow to the cause. Abraham

understands."

From the corner of the kitchen where he'd been leaning on the wall observing the argument, Abraham uncrossed his arms and stepped forward.

"No, Ruth, I don't."

Ruth turned in her chair to stare at him.

"What?" she asked in disbelief.

He sighed. "It was one thing when we were just standing there with our signs explaining our principles. But the violence today?" He shrugged. "It's been two months. Two months of no pay, Ruth! And for what? You saw Max Blanck's face today. He's not losing any sleep over workers picketing. Instead he's paying off cops to bash in heads. No, it's time to say we gave it our best and throw in the towel."

Ruth gaped at Abraham and looked to her father.

"Listen to the boy," he said, waving his hand.

"So, you want to betray the cause," she said softly.

Abraham put his hand on her shoulder, and she shrugged it off.

"Ruth, I've been very patient. You knew I was only doing this for you." He opened his arms to her, and she knew this was as close he'd get to begging for her to understand. "It's time to be smart. We can't continue starving our families for a losing cause.

They're offering double pay and forgiveness to anyone who crosses the picket line back to work. Think of that. We'd have enough to cover the family's expenses again and some leftover to bring my family over in no time."

Her eyes widened. "And lose our self-respect. That offer is just a bribe to cross the picket line! How long do you think that would last? How long until they treat us like dogs again?"

He sighed and turned away from her.

She stood from the table and shouted to his back. "We took a vow, Abraham! Does that mean nothing to you? Should I remember that when we say our own wedding vows?"

Abraham stared at the floor, refusing to meet her eye. He said in a soft whisper, "I never took the vow."

She reeled back in shock. "What?"

He looked up and shouted, "I didn't take the vow, Ruth!" He punched the wall in frustration. "Damn it! You knew I didn't want to get involved in this. I explained my reasons. But you had to be such a *noodge* about it."

She strode to him. "A *noodge*? I thought I was honoring our dead brothers and fighting for change." She poked him in the chest with her finger. "But 'scuse me. I didn't mean to be a *noodge* by forcing you to do the right thing."

Tatty's voice boomed. "Enough!"

They turned and looked at him in surprise.

"This has gone on long enough. Abraham defends you, but Ruth, you don't know. You're in over your head." Tatty wiped a hand over his haggard face. Spit clung to the corner of his mouth as he continued. "You think this is the worst violence they'll throw at you? A few paid-off cops? That's nothing."

Abraham looked at Tatty and opened his mouth to speak, but Tatty waved him off.

Ruth stepped closer to Tatty. "I might not have been on the front lines of Bloody Sunday, but I saw plenty, Tatty. I lived through the actual revolution while you two ran off to safety."

Tatty slammed his fist on the table. "Stop talking back! You think I don't know that?" His voice cracked and he gulped back a sob. "I hate myself for that. That's why I need to keep you safe now. These men are dangerous, Ruth. I can't lose another child."

Ruth stared in shock as tears spilled down Tatty's face. She'd made her father cry. She ran from the kitchen. She heard Tatty slam into his bedroom and Abraham's cot creak under his weight.

She threw herself on the couch and covered her head with a pillow as she heard the front door open. She heard Momme and Ester murmuring with Abraham. She waited for one of them to come in to check on her. But instead she heard the quiet squeaking of the bedroom door as Momme went to Tatty, and then the creaking of the cot as Ester sat down next to Abraham.

Ruth sat up, trying to understand what was happening. Was she being cast as the guilty party here? She was the noble one, fighting for a better future for Ester, honoring Momme's son and making his death mean something. Why was she the one sitting alone?

She faintly heard Ester cooing in a soothing voice and Abraham's ragged voice as he exclaimed, "She just doesn't understand!" With a guilty shudder, Ruth realized she'd made him cry also. She'd literally brought both the men in her life to tears.

"Ruth?"

She turned to see Samuel hovering awkwardly by the curtain in the doorway.

She wiped her face with the back of her hand.

"Oh, Samuel. I'm sorry. Please come sit down."

He sat on the edge of the couch next to her with

his hat clutched between his hands.

They sat in silence for a moment. Ruth racked her brain for something to say. He must hate her for making his son cry.

Samuel finally cleared his throat, glanced at the kitchen and spoke softly. "This is a difficult situation for everyone." He angled his body to look at her. "And believe it or not, we do understand how you are feeling. I don't even think you're wrong. But you're prioritizing the dead right now, Ruth."

She opened her mouth to defend herself, but he patted her knee.

"We all lost someone important to us that day. And it breaks my heart even further to think of all of you left behind in the aftermath." He shook his head and paused a moment to choose his next words. "Max Blanck isn't the czar. Defeating him will not bring back your brother. Just think on that."

He stood and walked from the room before she could say anything. In the silence left in his wake, she focused on Abraham speaking to Ester about the guilt he was carrying.

"I couldn't save them," he sobbed.

"Shh, no one expected you to," Ester said. "God spared you. We must be thankful for that."

Ruth stood and crept closer to the curtained doorway to hear them more clearly.

"I just couldn't live with myself if it happened again." He sniffed. "I can't watch Ruth die too, Ester. I wouldn't be able to go on."

Ester was silent. After a few moments she said, "She's stronger than you think."

Ruth smiled and backed away from her eavesdropping. Leave it to her sister to defend her and smooth the waves. Always the peacekeeper. Even as a child, she'd been the go-between when Ruth and Jeremiah fought. She and Jeremiah had been equally stubborn. Thick as walls, her mother said affectionately. At least some things stayed the same.

But hearing Abraham's confession of guilt gnawed at Ruth. He felt responsible. He wished he could've done more. She thought about what Samuel said about her prioritizing the dead. She looked out the window at the busy street below. The marketplace was buzzing with energy as usual. People on their way home from work were stopping to pick up dinner. Despite the atrocities on the picket line today, the city was unaffected. Was this the way the world worked? Evil could happen and life would just go on?

It was that way years ago when they were back

in Russia also. The czar's soldiers coming and ransacking their house. Dragging her mother out to the street for interrogation. Flopping Ester and Ruth about like rag dolls. Then after getting nothing from them, leaving the women to clean up the broken glass and belongings carelessly left behind. It was different, but exactly the same here.

Mirele and Zusa, despite their beatings today, were crammed into their crowded apartment, still sewing and washing clothes. Clara, Filomena and Chayele had been among the group arrested. Had they been released yet? The union had promised to put up the funds to post bail for everyone. How would she feel if she went back to work and something happened to one of them?

She was tired of moving on and pretending. She was tired of being considered too weak to matter. Samuel was wrong. She wasn't doing this for the dead. She was doing this for her friends. For the girls and women everywhere who were tired of being the victims. If Ruth abandoned them, they may never get a better future. They might not be the "living" Samuel wanted her to focus on, but she knew deep in her heart they needed her.

* * *

It was dark and Ester was sleeping on her side of the couch when Ruth slipped out from the blankets and got dressed the next morning. She heard Samuel's steady snores as she tiptoed into the kitchen. If she could make it without bumping any furniture, perhaps she could slip out the front door unnoticed. She didn't want to get in another argument about the picket line.

She was halfway to the door when she heard a match strike.

"Going somewhere?" Abraham was sitting at the kitchen table, fully dressed.

Ruth took a step closer to the door. "Please don't try and stop me. I don't want to fight anymore."

He sighed. "I'm not. I knew you'd go back."

"Then why are you up and dressed?" She gestured to his clothing.

He shrugged. "I might not agree, but I can't let you go alone. I promised to protect you, remember?"

"But you said you couldn't watch me get hurt again."

He got up, grabbed their coats and held hers out to her. "Then don't get hurt again, ya?"

She smiled and nodded. He opened the door and

gestured for her to go ahead of him. She patted him on the arm as she passed and they headed out side by side down the dark stairs into the cold morning air.

Abraham

It was cold. The wind whistled through the picket line. He looked down at his purpling fingers before tucking one hand in his coat pocket. With his other hand, he pulled Ruth closer to him, huddling their body heat together.

Yankel sauntered over. "Need a nip?" He offered Abraham his metal flask with a wink. Abraham smiled and took it. The whiskey burned his throat on the way down and offered a spark of warmth that spread through his chest.

"Thanks." Abraham said. "I needed that."

Yankel nodded and took another sip himself. He then offered it to Ruth, who shook her head. Abraham knew she couldn't stand the taste of alcohol. Abraham reached over her head and took the offered flask back from Yankel for himself.

This had to be one of the worst days. They'd all been cold. But this was a whole other extreme. It had to be below zero. They were also still bruised and sore from the attack two days ago. The police officers stood watch nearby, their mere presence a looming threat.

The sound of a car turning onto the block drew his attention. Please, oh please don't be Max Blanck again. Abraham couldn't possibly stand the sight of him today. But surprisingly, another car followed the first. Then another and another. Abraham turned to Yankel with wide eyes. What was happening?

The line of cars pulled to a stop in front of the Triangle and well-dressed women in fur coats and elaborate hats poured out with swishing skirts. They carried piles of blankets and began distributing them among the crowd of workers. Two other women directed their drivers to set up a table, where they set up hot beverage carafes and baskets of food.

Abraham heard Clara exclaim from nearby, "What is this? The Mink Brigade?"

"No, they're angels," another girl said.

When a plate of food and a hot cup of coffee was handed to Abraham a few minutes later, he didn't care if they'd come from the Devil himself. He accepted gratefully and said a prayer of thanks for whatever miracle brought these ladies to the picket line that day.

* * *

With a full belly and a blanket over his shoulders, Abraham felt like a king. Yankel stood next to him and pointed out other items on the table he wanted to try.

"Ooh look, they have cookies. And hot chocolate. Next time I definitely want the hot chocolate."

Abraham couldn't help but smile at his friend. How did he manage to keep such a positive attitude? Maybe his secret was to think with his stomach.

Chayele strode over. "You should be ashamed!"

Yankel turned. "Why? Because I like chocolate?"

She shot him a glare. "You're letting them buy your trust. For all you know they're friends of Max Blanck's, here to spy on us."

Yankel scoffed. "Oy, you've been listening to Clara too much. She's turning you into one of her conspiracy nuts."

Suddenly, Abraham heard Ruth speaking behind him. All three of them turned to look at Ruth standing with the women clustered around her.

"She couldn't have been more than twelve."

"You say he was forcing himself on her?" one heavyset woman with huge eyebrows asked. "You're sure she wasn't offering herself?"

"Of course she wasn't," Ruth sputtered. "She was terrified and screaming while he held her down."

"What is she doing?" Chayele whispered.

Abraham hurried to Ruth's side. He took in the discomfited expressions of the women standing there. How they pulled their fur coats tighter and fiddled with their pearls. Ruth, however, had a hardened stance. She stood rigid with her chin up, almost daring them to challenge her.

He grabbed her elbow. "Ruth, a word?"

She shook him off and kept speaking. "There are others also. Other young girls that work in the factory. I've seen them."

The heavyset woman with huge eyebrows stared hard at Ruth. She looked like she was concentrating deeply on something. Finally she gestured for Ruth to follow her as she walked to the reporters.

Ruth moved to follow the woman and Abraham pulled her back.

"What are you doing? You cannot tell a reporter this story!"

"They're asking for the truth." She hurried after the woman and he watched as she was introduced to the reporters and they opened their notebooks.

Yankel came up next to Abraham. "What are you going to do, Abe? If that story includes her name, Max Blanck will know exactly who to blame."

Abraham groaned and rushed over to where Ruth stood with the reporters, but she was already spelling her name to them.

"The girl was definitely not consenting?"

"No, she was screaming," Ruth repeated.

Abraham clapped his hand over the reporter's notebook. "Please don't use her name. You can't reveal her as the source!"

The reporter glared at Abraham and pulled his notebook away to continue writing. "I'll see what I can do, but it'll be up to my editor."

It was too late. The bottle had been uncorked. Why couldn't Ruth see the danger she was unearthing?

* * *

He'd been right. He hated that he was, but that didn't change anything. The article, quoting Ruth extensively, came out the next day. And it caused a stir. Neighbors stopped by all day expressing surprise and wonder at Ruth's bravery. Abba and Jacob laid into him, telling him what a failure he was in protecting his future wife.

Ruth, on the other hand, seemed unaffected. "The story needed to be told. They needed to hear our side with the full details. If it made people uncomfortable, it worked."

"But you directly poked the bear! Max Blanck now knows *your* name specifically."

Ruth chewed her lip. She finally looked a little less sure.

They stayed home from the picket line for a few days, but Yankel reported no sightings of looming thugs. Just more food and hot chocolate.

So, Abraham and Ruth finally left the apartment. His body was tense and on high alert the entire time; he stiffened at every noise and shadow along the way. A week went by, but Max Blanck did not respond. In fact, he was not seen in public for days. Had Ruth been right? Had the risk been worth it?

He watched her sipping a cup of hot chocolate one day, laughing with her friends. Where did her strength come from? He knew some of her action that day had come more from her impulsivity than truly understanding the risk she was taking. Still, she had seen Clara's bloody, bruised face, and Ruth was far from stupid. She knew what Max Blanck was capable of. And she'd spoken up anyway.

Abraham liked to believe his hesitation was because of the risks he feared Ruth was taking—inadvertent or not. But he knew if Jeremiah were here, he'd call him out on what might be the real truth.

Abraham was afraid.

Maybe there was a reason he kept being drawn to risktakers. As much as he enjoyed living in the shadows undetected, he also appreciated the buzz of adrenaline. Who knew what lay ahead, but with Ruth by his side, he knew there'd be adventure. He just hoped it wouldn't lead to regrets.

R u t h

Ruth's frozen fingers curled around the cup of hot chocolate in her hand. She bent her face over the cup and breathed in the steam. She held her elbows out in a protective stance to prevent anyone from banging into her and spilling the precious beverage.

"Drink up quick. It won't stay warm long," Chayele said, coming up behind her.

"Then I'll just get a refill." Ruth took a small sip.

Chayele snorted. "Provided they stick around."

Ruth rolled her eyes at Chayele's cynicism. She knew Chayele's feelings on the Mink Brigade were spurred on by Clara. Clara believed no rich person could ever understand the problems of poor people, and they were only there to support the garment workers for their own excitement and notoriety.

Ever since the article, Ruth felt some loyalty to the Mink Brigade. They had to care about the girls for real after that, right? And the article wouldn't have been published if they hadn't used their connections. She felt Chayele and Clara should be more grateful.

Ruth glanced at her fellow picketers. Was it her imagination, or were there fewer girls than yesterday? The numbers kept dropping, despite their steadfast slogan, "We'd rather starve quick than starve slow." It was the middle of February, the fourth month on the picket line, and they had very little to show for it.

As Ruth took her cup back to the beverage station, she noticed a car pulling up. The demonstrators sprang to life, yelling to catch the occupants' attention. The few remaining reporters scribbled in their notebooks. The car door opened and out stepped Lemon Face and Skinny Beanpole. A hush fell over the picket line as they approached the crowd. This was the first time any of the union leaders had visited the picket line. Until now, they'd kept to the union office, handling everything behind the scenes.

The reporters began an assault of questions.

"Any news of a resolution?"

"Have you communicated with Mr. Blanck?"

Skinny Beanpole held out a hand to wave off the reporters. "We are here to speak with our workers. Please allow us to do so."

The reporters fell silent, but elbowed closer to the picket line.

Those on the line were silent. Mirele and Zusa held their breath and dropped their signs as they grabbed for each other. Abraham came up behind Ruth and slung an arm around her shoulder. She looked up and patted his hand.

The men exchanged a look before Lemon Face cleared his throat and spoke. "The strike is over."

The picket line erupted with cheers. Hats flew up into the air as the crowd celebrated.

"Wait! Wait!" Skinny Beanpole shouted. "You need to listen!"

A few minutes passed before the excitement

subsided and his voice cracked as he continued. "We were unable to come to a resolution with Mr. Blanck."

"Then how is the strike over?" shouted a cutter from the back of the crowd.

Lemon Face ignored the question. "You will go back to work. The union is no longer supporting you."

"What does that mean?" Clara shouted.

Chayele shouted. "What about our raise?"

"Mr. Blanck agreed to increase your wages by two dollars and to pay for electricity and needles," Lemon Face responded. "But your hours will not be cut."

"But the other factories agreed to shorter hours!"

"And what did you mean the union is no longer supporting us?" yelled another girl.

A man spoke, "What about the safety concerns?"

Ruth felt uneasiness creeping up her spine. All around her, people murmured and gestured angrily. The union leaders, sensing the crowd turning against them, begged frantically for quiet.

"As we said, there won't be a resolution." Skinny Beanpole's face was red and sweat beaded on his forehead despite the cold. He tugged on his collar. "You want a job; you got a job—work starts tomorrow. But he'll only have an in-house union from here on out. Go to them with any further concerns."

The men turned and walked back to the car.

"That's it?" Chayele shouted. "You're leaving us?"

They ignored her cries and picked up their pace. The crowd pushed the barriers away and ran after them. Seeing the crowd gaining, the men sprinted to their car and ducked inside. The crowd descended, screaming and banging on the windows and doors of the car as it pulled away from the curb. Abraham pulled Ruth's arm and they turned to leave the chaos behind. Out of the corner of her eye, Ruth watched the Mink Brigade pack up their cars.

* * *

Ruth swirled the cabbage soup in her bowl with her spoon, ignoring her mother's anxious stare. She knew she had barely touched her dinner, but she didn't care. Ever since the union leaders made the announcement, Ruth felt like there was a chunk of coal sitting in her stomach. Her family had tried to talk to her when she got home, but she couldn't muster up any responses to their attempts to look on the positive side.

There was no positive side—how could they not see that? They were folding. Giving up without gaining even a quarter of their demands. The only upside she could see in the whole mess was that Abraham and her father had somehow managed to restrain themselves from saying "I told you so."

A knock at the door disrupted Ruth's moping. Samuel got up to answer it.

"Is Miss Feldman here?"

Ruth looked up at the sound of her name.

"Who's asking?" Samuel asked.

"Mr. Blanck sent me. He wants to speak with her."

Ruth got up from the table and went to see who was speaking. It was a man in a buttoned jacket with a pinched expression. She recognized the uniform—it was Mr. Blanck's driver. He drew back and extracted a handkerchief from his breast pocket to wipe his hand after touching the door.

Abraham and Tatty stood and looked at the man over her head.

"What does he want with her?" Abraham asked.

The driver stepped back even farther from the door. "My instructions were to escort her to the factory, sir. That's all I was told."

The three men exchanged nervous glances as Ruth put on her coat. Her insides felt like they were doing somersaults. Good thing she hadn't eaten.

"You're actually going to go?" Tatty asked.

She gestured at the driver. "We can't leave him standing there."

Abraham grabbed his coat. "I'm going with you."

Ruth smiled gratefully. She felt stronger with him.

Tatty crossed his arms and glared. "This could be a trap. Blanck wants revenge for the article."

Ruth rolled her eyes. "Yes, his driver is going to drive us out of the city and dispose of us."

The driver harrumphed and looked at the floor.

"No good can come of this." Tatty scowled.

She patted him on the shoulder. "Only one way to find out," she said, trying to keep her voice steady. She pecked him on the cheek and strode out the door with Abraham behind.

She slammed to a stop on the sidewalk, though, when she saw the limo waiting at the curb. Perhaps Tatty's suspicious nature was rubbing off on her. Max Blanck was not a generous or frivolous man. In fact, she'd classify him as extremely calculating. So, why was he sending his best car, as well as his driver, to fetch her after hours? Ruth glanced nervously at Abraham. He took her hand and gave it a squeeze as they ducked into the backseat of the luxurious car.

They pulled up to the curb outside the Triangle Factory ten minutes later. Ruth's heart pounded as the driver escorted them into the darkened building. She'd never before seen the interior so quiet and dimly lit. She felt like a trespasser intruding upon the eerie calm. They entered the foyer, and the driver directed them to the elevators.

The elevator operator, Joseph, greeted them with a shy smile and nod. Ruth had seen Joseph and the other elevator operator, Gaspar, around the factory, but hadn't spoken to him again since her first day. She wondered if he remembered her. Since that day, she'd joined the rest of the factory workers who took the stairs, leaving the elevators for the owners and the rest of their administrative staff on the executive floor.

Both Joseph and Gaspar greeted the staff in the lobby each day with kind smiles and small talk about the weather or newsworthy events. She always appreciated that they made the effort. It demonstrated that although they rubbed elbows with the executives all day, they still aligned themselves with the workers.

She stepped into the elevator and her eyes again swept over every plush detail as the contraption soared upwards. She felt the spark of anger ignite inside her. Blanck and the other rich folk on the upper floors got to surround themselves in luxury while crushing their workers down into nothing.

She turned to Joseph. "How do you do it?"

He blinked. "Do what, Miss?"

"Stand beside them and smile all day? Treat them with respect, when they're so awful?"

Joseph shifted his weight and looked away without answering. The elevator dinged as they reached the tenth floor and he pulled open the gate. As she moved to leave, she felt his hand on her arm.

"I just remember, I'm the one operating the controls," he said.

It took her a second to understand what he meant. Then Ruth laughed and marveled at this man's insight. Her tension loosened. She looked over at Abraham and he squeezed her hand.

"Good luck, Miss," Joseph said, tipping his hat.

She took a deep breath and stepped out to the empty administrative floor. An office light shone in the distance—just like the night she'd walked in on Grosevich with the girl. She shuddered.

Abraham frowned and tugged her to the lit office. "Let's get this over with."

She bit her lip as they neared the office and she saw Max Blanck through the glass window, sitting and scribbling furiously at his desk. He looked up at the sound of their approach and leapt to his feet.

"Miss Feldman. And Mr. Reznik! Nice to see you also. How good of you to accept my invitation." He gestured to the chairs in front of his desk. "Please, come and sit."

Ruth and Abraham exchanged a look and lowered themselves into the two seats facing his desk. Ruth folded her hands in her lap, trying to steady her right leg from twitching and her foot tapping on the floor.

Mr. Blanck sat back down and looked at them. His lips curved into a grin.

"It's been quite a few months, hasn't it?" He leaned back in his chair and crossed his arms behind his head. "A very trying time, I must say. So much to do and deal with. I don't believe I've gotten a good night's sleep in weeks."

He slapped his hands on his desk. "But, enough about me." He opened his desk drawer and withdrew a folded newspaper. "I wanted to applaud your contributions in person, Miss Feldman."

Ruth relinquished any hope of control over her nervous tapping. She dug her wrist into her thigh in a last attempt to steady it.

He gestured at her with the newspaper. "I'm a huge believer that true strength comes from the individual, not the masses." He unfolded the newspaper and smoothed it out on his desk. "Although the picket line gained attention, not much about it actually stood out. But your article, Miss Feldman? That drew attention."

He paused and surveyed her. She tried to breathe evenly. He flexed his hands over the article on the desk and smiled—savoring the moment and his command of power, she guessed.

Abraham put his hands on the edge of the desk. "What do you want exactly, Mr. Blanck?"

"Ah, yes. I guess it is getting late." Mr. Blanck said. "My point is this: The masses were easy to quash. But there are a few individuals who I wish to handle a bit differently. More personally, if you will."

He got to his feet and came around to lean on the front of the desk, inches away from Ruth.

"I want you to be one of my new union leaders."

"What?" Ruth gasped.

"I'm setting up our own in-house union. I want you to be one of the leaders. You know, to handle workers' complaints and such."

Ruth frowned. "One of your puppets, you mean."

He chuckled and looked at Abraham. "She does speak her mind, doesn't she?"

"I'm not going to spy for you." Ruth crossed her arms in front of her. "I'm not going to make a mockery of what is supposed to be an organization representing the rights of workers."

"You'd get a promotion as well. Back to the finishing table. And your training would be paid this time." He smiled and looked to Abraham again.

"As it should always be. But my answer is still no." She stood and turned away from him.

"I don't think you realize the situation you're in." His voice was like steel. "This isn't really a choice."

Abraham got to his feet and took a step to Ruth. "If she doesn't take your offer?"

Mr. Blanck shrugged. "She loses her job. I make sure no other factory in the city will hire her. Same for you and her little sister."

Ruth turned back to him, her mouth agape.

Mr. Blanck moved back around his desk and picked up a pile of papers. "Oh, and her friends too. Those four girls she sits with." He winked. "Not really a choice, is it?"

Ruth choked back a sob.

"What if I took the position?" Abraham asked.

A smile spread across Mr. Blanck's face. "Interesting. She speaks her mind and you cover her tracks? You'd better watch the precedent you're setting for this marriage."

"Enough," Abraham thundered. Then he swallowed hard and lowered his voice. "Promote me to a collar and leave her be." His face was dark red.

Mr. Blanck nodded. "Keep her—all of them—in line. Any disruptions and you're out, you understand?"

Abraham straightened his shoulders and nodded. "*Farshtanen*. Got your message loud and clear, sir."

Mr. Blanck dropped the paper he was holding and glared at Abraham. The two stood, gazes locked for a moment. Finally, he looked back to his desk again.

"Have Joseph take you downstairs. My driver will take you home. You'll begin your new position tomorrow, Reznik."

Abraham turned and grabbed Ruth's arm. His fingers dug in as he swept her from the office. He strode to the elevators, but Ruth pulled away and ran to the stairs instead. She barreled down; teeth clenched. Abraham came behind. He caught her on the landing and swung her up against the wall.

"What is wrong with you? You're mad at *me*?"

She choked out a sob. "How could you give in?"

"To protect you, Ruth. He gave us no choice."

She pushed him away. "There's always a choice."

She took off running again. Behind her, she heard him slam his fist into the wall and curse.

Ester

"Oy, I'm stuffed!" Ester put down her fork with a smile. The taste of chocolate still coated her tongue.

Across the table, Tatty wiped his mouth with a napkin and pushed his own plate to the side. "A feast fit for the girl we celebrate!" he said with a grin.

Momme clapped her hands. "Wait, there's more!" Everyone groaned together. Samuel leaned back with his hand on his stomach. "I'll be loosening my belt soon, Rachel."

"Not more food." She swatted Samuel. "Ester's present!"

A present! Ester couldn't remember the last time she'd received a birthday present, although Momme had always found a way to celebrate their birthdays. Even during the hardest times in Russia, Momme would somehow scrounge up a loaf of bread or a slice of meat to help them feel special. But this year, she'd really outdone herself. A meal of all Ester's favorites and a decadent chocolate cake. And now a present?

Momme produced a package wrapped in cheesecloth and presented it to Ester. "For your first real American birthday."

"We were here last year," Ester protested.

Momme waved her words away and sat back at the table. "Eh, it was all still new. Now you're settled, embracing your future."

Ester understood the true meaning behind Momme's words and her quick, private wink—she was pleased, or at least accepting, of Ester's decision to join the Jewish Teacher's program. Ester glanced at Tatty and Ruth. Had Momme told them about their conversation? Ruth was tapping her fingers, like she was eager to be go somewhere and her sister's birthday was holding her up.

"Open it!" Abraham jutted his chin to her gift.

Ester's fingers shook as she unwrapped it. Inside was a leather-bound book of blank pages.

"It's a journal," Momme explained. "I thought you could use it to document your new American life."

Ester jumped to her feet and ran to Momme and gathered her in a hug. "I love it, *a sheynem dank*!"

Momme patted Ester's back, "Of course, *bubbele*. I hope you fill it with nothing but joy."

Ester kissed Momme's cheek. "God-willing."

She returned to her seat and Ruth rose to gather dishes. "Wait," Momme said, gesturing for Ruth to sit back down. "There's still more. Your father and I have an announcement."

Ester smiled to herself, reveling in being the first to know what was coming.

Momme reached for Tatty's hand. He looked to her and smiled. Momme took a deep breath. "We're having a baby!"

"*Mazel Tov!*" Samuel said, leaping to his feet. He kissed both Momme and Tatty on the cheeks.

Abraham patted Tatty on the back.

Ruth sidled over to Ester and whispered, "Did you know this?"

Ester nodded.

At Ruth's hurt expression, Ester said, "Didn't you notice the signs? Momme only confirmed it when I questioned her about it."

Ruth bristled in response. "Well, I've been a bit occupied lately, coming off the picket line and all."

Ester put her hand on Ruth's arm. "It doesn't matter who she told first. She's sharing it now."

After a moment, Ruth nodded. She moved to gather Momme in a hug. Ester smiled.

"Nice job, there," Abraham said from behind her. She turned to see him crouched by her chair.

"I just calmed the ruffled feathers," Ester said.

"So, was your birthday everything you dreamed?"

"And more."

"Good. If anyone deserves to feel special, it's you," Abraham said. He reached into his pocket. "I made you something." He slid a small wrapped package onto the table in front of her.

"Oh, Abraham, you shouldn't have." She pulled at the tied twine and the cloth fell away to reveal a beautiful carved bird.

He shrugged awkwardly. "It just came to me and I knew it was meant for you. Happy birthday!"

Ester felt her cheeks heat up. She was about to thank him when Abraham rose to his feet.

"Excuse me," he said, moving to where Samuel and Tatty were waving for him.

Ester noticed Ruth grabbing her coat by the door.

"Goodbye! *Mazel Tov* again!" she shouted.

"Wait! We're about to play cards." Momme cried.

Ruth shrugged. "I'm meeting the girls. Ester understands, right?"

Ester shifted uncomfortably in her seat as everyone looked at her. She gave a small nod just so everyone would stop staring at her.

With another quick wave, Ruth was gone.

Momme's mouth was a hard line. "The gall of that girl," Momme said to Tatty. "You must speak with her."

"And say what, exactly?" he asked. "That she must stay home and be with the family?"

"She needs direction, guidance."

"I've offered all that. I've tried forbidding her— remember how well that went?"

Samuel and Abraham crept to the coat rack and grabbed their coats. Samuel gestured to his pipe. "We'll just give you a moment"

Left alone with her parent's bickering, Ester felt her own anger at Ruth begin to boil. It was her birthday! Couldn't Ruth choose her for once? With one careless wave, she'd changed the entire dynamic of the evening. Ester refused to give Ruth that power.

"Enough!" Ester shouted.

Her parents shushed and turned to her.

"Ruth can make her own decisions. If anything, you need to leave it between her and Abraham. But can we please enjoy the rest of the evening?"

Momme blushed and looked down to the plate she was holding. She nodded.

Tatty pulled out a chair and sat back down across from Ester. "Of course, *sheifale,* I apologize."

Ester played with the handle of the teacup in front of her. Momme walked the plate over to the sink.

"I actually need to speak to you about something, since we have privacy for once," Tatty said.

Ester leaned into the table and folded her hands.

"You're officially fifteen today." Tatty twisted the napkin on the table in front of him. "That means you have a choice about school."

"Oh," Ester said. "I hadn't even thought of that." She'd assumed she'd continue on at school as she had been. She'd applied for evening classes at the Jewish Teacher's College so they wouldn't interfere.

"Well, I know you were unhappy about me forcing you to attend school. It's up to you now, if you continue."

"That seems like so long ago. I've grown more comfortable with English and am finally settling in."

Tatty continued fidgeting with the napkin. "But if you wanted to work…well, I wouldn't stop you."

"Do *you* want me to work?" Ester asked.

Tatty shifted in his chair. "With the baby coming…"

Momme stepped back over to the table and put a hand on Tatty's shoulder. "We are not putting pressure on you. We know you have important plans." She shot Tatty a look.

Tatty fidgeted in his seat. "Ya, your mother told me about the program. And I couldn't be prouder. My daughter, a teacher in America!" He twisted his hands. "But things will be tight. The baby, still saving for Samuel and Abraham's family to come…"

Momme spoke. "That's not Ester's responsibility."

Ester waved a hand to Momme and reached across the table to Tatty. "I'd be happy to help. Everyone has always stepped up to care for me. I'd be honored to do my part now to contribute."

Tatty looked up with shimmering eyes. "You're too good, *sheifale.*"

Ester smiled and stood to gather plates from the

table. Momme scurried to Ester's side and took the plates from Ester. "It's your birthday. You can't clean dishes tonight!"

"But you can't do them yourself!"

Momme laughed. "Of course I can. Go, play cards with your father. You two never get time alone."

Ester put a hand on Momme's arm. "Thank you Momme. It was a beautiful dinner." She picked up her journal. "And I can't wait to begin writing."

Ester joined her father in the parlor, where he was already shuffling cards. From the kitchen came the sounds of water running and Momme humming to herself. Tatty smiled as he dealt out the cards. The warmth of the moment enveloped her. Ruth may have left, but her birthday was still turning out to be perfect.

R u t h

Saturday May 14th, 1910

313 Days Until the Fire

The spring sun beckoned as Ruth waited behind her friends to have her bag inspected. It was a beautiful Saturday in May and the weekend unfolded before her with inviting prospects. But the guards were taking even more time than usual to poke through bags.

"What is this, the Inquisition or something?" Chayele shouted. "Lay off, you're performing purse inspections not shakedowns!"

One of the guards looked up and sneered at her before returning to the bag he was searching.

Filomena reached over and patted Chayele on the

arm. "The beautiful day will still be there."

"Ya, just not the sun," Chayele grumbled. "They've gotten more obnoxious since the strike. Did anything good come from that?"

Ruth shrugged. "Two more dollars a week?"

They chuckled, but they'd had similar exchanges often over the past three months. Very little had changed since the strike. It was a raw subject.

Ester's voice piped up from behind them. "Shouldn't you just be happy you still have jobs?"

Chayele whirled around. "You sure have a lot to say for someone who wasn't there."

Ruth scowled, and Ester closed her mouth. This was not the first time Ester stepped on someone's toes.

Chayele turned back to Ruth and shot her an exasperated look before changing the subject. Ruth sighed. She knew the girls only tolerated Ester's comments because of their friendship with her. Why couldn't Ester just keep her mouth shut? And how did she even come to hold such opinions, for that matter?

The line moved forward finally, bringing them face to face with the guards. The sneering guard locked eyes with Chayele, and then emptied the contents of her purse on the floor. Chayele lurched forward, while Filomena and Zusa grabbed her by the arms.

"Let it go, Chayele," Filomena begged.

The guard let out a laugh, and his partner gave him a hearty pat on the back.

"That'll teach you, huh *Chaya?*" he growled.

The guards walked away, while the girls dropped to the floor to gather Chayele's belongings.

Chayele blinked a few times and flipped her hair over her shoulder, revealing the scar on her temple. The others looked away, pretending not to see. Ruth remembered the day she'd gotten the scar. They'd been arrested on the picket line.

Chayele had refused to cry in front of the police officers. As she was entering the jail cell, one of them hit her on the side of the head and asked her if she'd cry now. She had blood dripping into her eyes from the cut he gave her, but barely released a whimper. Ruth cried like a baby when they got to her.

Ester picked up the last hair pin and handed it to Chayele, who frowned but accepted it wordlessly before getting to her feet and cracking a half-smile.

"Let's catch the last of that sunlight." she said.

The girls nodded and took off for the stairs. Despite the incident and the tension radiating off Chayele, Ruth was in a good mood. It had been a pretty easy week at the factory. The weather was finally great. She was even pondering asking Abraham to go out with her to the movies this evening. Maybe they could pump some fun back into this engagement of theirs. She tilted her head back and laughed as Filomena finished the punch line of a joke and pushed the front door open with Chayele.

They both looked up and came to a slamming halt.

Standing across the street from the factory was the heavyset woman from the Mink Brigade. Ruth hadn't seen her since the last day of the strike.

Hundreds of regrets and memories swept through Ruth's mind. The article would never have been published if it hadn't been for that woman. Abraham wouldn't have been blackmailed into becoming union leader. And she and Abraham wouldn't have spent months barely on speaking terms. She scowled at the woman. It felt good to have someone to blame.

The woman stepped forward. Ruth exchanged looks with Chayele and the rest of the girls. She knew her friends also harbored anger against the woman and her friends, who had abandoned them when the union leaders folded. Clara had been right. The Mink Brigade, like everyone else, seemed to forget about the factory workers and their hardships just as soon as the strike was out of the news.

Ester, oblivious to the tension, skipped off to greet Abraham, who stood on the corner talking with Yankel. Ruth looked after her, envying her ignorance.

"Ruth?" The woman smiled. "Just the girl I was looking for! We were never formally introduced, but I'm Anne Morgan."

Ruth ignored the woman's outstretched hand. "Why are you looking for me?"

Anne appeared startled by Ruth's hostility. But tucking her hand away, she continued, "I'm hoping we can renew our alliance."

Chayele pushed past Ruth to confront Anne. "Why should we put ourselves out for you after all of you abandoned us?"

"Abandoned you? Whatever do you mean?"

"When the strike ended." Chayele scowled. "You and your Mink Brigade friends cleared out of here without a backward glance."

"What would you have had us do? The union leaders settled." Anne gestured to the building behind them. "Max Blanck shut down any further chance for negotiation. What pull did you believe we had? We were only volunteers fighting for the cause, like you."

"But the reporter," Ruth sputtered.

"That was all you. Your courage to speak the

truth." Anne patted Ruth's arm. "I just brought him over to you."

"But if he liked the story, why didn't they report the end of the strike?" Filomena asked.

Anne laughed. "You honestly believe a man like Max Blanck would allow any more negative press? He's a man with deep pockets and a fierce temper."

She reached into her bag and took out a handful of papers. "But these reasons are why I need you girls to join me now. To take down powerful people like Max Blanck, we need to go over his head."

Ruth saw Chayele lift a skeptical eyebrow. Ruth glanced over her shoulder at Abraham and Ester. Abraham was shifting his weight from one foot to the other, his pockets bulged from his hands fisted inside. She turned back to Anne and accepted the flier the woman handed her. But looking down at it, she could not read any of the English words printed across the page. Despite becoming more comfortable speaking the language, she still had yet to find Abraham-approved sources to practice reading.

"Miss Morgan, I don't know what you're looking for here." She thrust the paper back into Anne's hands. "But we're not in a position to get involved with any of your activities right now. We have work each day and little time to spare."

Anne clasped Ruth's hand as she turned away. "But the factory is closed on Sundays, is it not? Which means you are free tomorrow."

* * *

Ruth slammed the front door behind her. "Why didn't you wait for me?" she demanded.

"You were taking too long." Abraham yawned and turned a page of the *Jewish Daily Forward* spread before him on the table. "I didn't feel like waiting for you to finish *schmoozing* with some rich *shiksa*."

She crossed her arms. "What about your promise to Tatty?"

He shrugged. "Ester needed me to walk her home. You seemed to be in safe hands with your friends."

She exhaled a deep breath. She was not getting into another fight with him. Not tonight. She could perhaps still salvage her plans for this evening.

She sat in the chair across from him at the table. "Do you want to hear what we were speaking about?"

He didn't look up from the newspaper. "Not really. I somehow figure anything concerning that woman will only make me upset."

She reached across the table and cupped her hand

over his. "Please Abraham, I'm trying to include you."

He frowned, but folded the newspaper in half on the table in front of him. "Fine, Ruth, what did you speak about? But before you share, remember you promised you wouldn't cause any further disturbances in the factory. I'm still indebted to Mr. Blanck."

She rolled her eyes. "This has nothing to do with the factory. I'm joining the suffragettes and marching in the parade tomorrow for women's rights."

"A suffragette parade?" He pinched the bridge of his nose. "Ruth, don't you ever stop?"

He stood and walked to the door.

Ruth rose to follow him. "Where are you going? I thought we could do something together tonight."

He turned back to face her. "Ruth, you promised this was over. Yet I know you're still meeting with Clara and the others, planning and plotting. And now the suffragettes? I just can't, Ruth. I'm going to go meet Yankel. Don't wait up."

He grabbed his hat off the hook and slammed out the door. Ruth was left staring at the closed door, clenching and unclenching her fists helplessly.

An hour later, Ruth sat on the couch in the parlor, plunging a needle through the ripped hemline of her gray skirt. Anne had said to wear white or the lightest color they owned as a way to distinguish the supporters of the cause. She couldn't believe she was spending her evening off at home, sewing. She'd hoped Abraham would return soon after he'd cooled off, but that didn't seem to be the case.

"May I come in, Ruth?" Ester stood in the doorway.

Ruth shrugged. "It's your room too."

Ester skittered across to the chair by the window.

Ruth sighed. "I know you heard everything, Ester. You don't have to avoid me."

Ester lifted her gaze halfway and cleared her throat. "I just don't want you to be angry with me."

"Because you disagree also?" Ruth frowned.

Ester chewed on a fingernail and looked down at her lap. "I worry about you being manipulated, Ruth."

"Manipulated?" Ruth dropped her skirt in her lap and looked up at Ester. "How?"

"What do you know about this woman? Why didn't she check up on you after the article was printed?" Ester's voice shook. "Mr. Blanck could have sent thugs after you like he did to Clara Lemlich. You were lucky, but she didn't know that. She pushed you into sharing that story with the press and left you to deal with the consequences."

Ruth looked down to her lap and picked up her skirt again with unsteady fingers.

"She knew I could handle it," she mumbled. "She said I was strong, called me a born leader."

Ester picked up her chair and tentatively moved it closer to Ruth. "A born leader for what exactly? What does she want from you?"

"Why do her intentions have to be suspect? I'm not worth someone's attention?"

Ester held up her hands. "I'm not saying that. It's just—you must see your life is very different from hers. She has little to lose, while you could lose everything."

Ruth mulled over Ester's words. *Was* she being manipulated? Flattered? But Anne seemed so sincere. She'd driven Ruth home so they could speak in private, and complimented her on being brave enough to speak out against Mr. Blanck and the Triangle's shady practices. She'd even given Ruth advice on handling her difficulties at home.

"Give your fiancé time and he'll come around," Anne had said, leaning her head back on the plush leather car seat. "He just needs to understand how important this is to you. If he cares for you the way you believe he does, he'll support you and you'll find a compromise that works."

Listening to her words of hope and wisdom, Ruth had been able to breathe easily for the first time in weeks. She believed Anne, and been ready to give Abraham the space he needed until he came around. But now with Ester staring her down and questioning Anne's motives, Ruth wasn't so sure.

A smug smile spread across Ester's lips, and Ruth's moment of uncertainty passed.

She threw her sewing down. "What do you know of any of this? You've just become Tatty and Abraham's puppet, repeating everything they say over the dinner table."

"I do not! Just because I agree with them doesn't mean I'm not forming my own opinions. I lived through the revolution too, Ruth. I saw the damage it caused."

"Then how can you be so blind? That young girl I saw being attacked was your age! Younger even!" Ruth swallowed and took a deep breath. She managed to lower her voice. "You're a young woman with every American freedom at your fingertips. You have a voice. You're growing up with democracy. Yet you refuse to take advantage of it all. Why?"

Ester scowled. "Because I refuse to be selfish."

"Selfish?" Ruth gasped. "How am I selfish?"

"We lived through hell in Russia. But that was

out of our control. We couldn't avoid the chaos—the czar, the government. But *you*—you're seeking out this fight. You're making our lives difficult."

"Sometimes things have to become more difficult before they can get better." Ruth gestured to the window, the city outside.

"I already did difficult. I'm done with difficult." Ester plucked at her skirt in her lap. "After surviving what we did in Russia, I just want life to be simple."

Ruth stared at her for a minute before turning away. What could she say to that? She had to admit, Ester had a point.

From behind her, she heard Ester clear her throat. "Abraham feels the same way, Ruth."

Ruth jerked her head up. "How do you know what Abraham feels?"

"I listen to him—something you should be doing! It's not fair what you're doing to him. He's too good a man to be dragged into these fights against his will."

"Back off Ester, you're crossing the line now," Ruth sputtered.

"Fine!" Ester shrugged and stalked out the room. "Ignore me. That seems to be all you do these days."

✳ ✳ ✳

Later that night, Ruth woke to the click of the front door and heard Abraham's quiet footsteps cross the kitchen floor. She slid off the couch and wrapped her shawl around her shoulders. Ester lifted her head up from her pillow and whispered in a sleepy voice, "You better apologize and not pick another fight."

"It's not your business, remember?" Ruth snapped.

Ester sighed and flipped to her other side.

Ruth shuffled into the kitchen, where Abraham stood over the sink gulping down a glass of water.

"Where were you?" she whispered. "I was worried."

He shrugged. "Out. I needed to clear my head."

She stepped closer to him. "About tomorrow."

He held up a hand, stopping her. "I'll walk you there and pick you up. But that's it. I'm not staying and we're not speaking of this again."

He looked so beaten down and tired. She knew she was responsible for imposing this strain on him. She should feel badly. But all she felt was excitement that he was allowing her to participate in the parade.

"Thank you, Abraham," she whispered.

He nodded and sat down on his cot next to Samuel's sleeping form. She watched as he removed his shoes, and without even changing out of his clothes, lay back to sleep.

They left for the parade the next morning in silence. The warm sunshine danced on her shoulders and she tilted her face up to the sky to enjoy it, while Abraham pulled his hat down lower to block it out. She put her hand on his arm in a comforting gesture, but he yanked away and quickened his pace. Ruth trailed behind, practically running to keep up.

As they neared the starting place for the parade, the crowds grew larger. Abraham walked in front with his elbows out, clearing a pathway. Beautiful women dressed in white and decorated with pins and banners handed out fliers. Straight ahead was a line of cars with a large group standing in front. Ruth recognized Anne and Chayele and waved to get their attention. Anne had said the cars were meant to be the focal point of the parade. The suffragettes were trying to illustrate the point that if women were capable of driving, why shouldn't they be capable of voting? Anne saw Ruth and waved.

"Go ahead," Abraham grunted. "I'll be back in three hours."

Ruth nodded. She knew he was telling her she'd better be waiting for him. She made a mental note to watch the time; she couldn't take another fight this weekend. She scurried off to meet everyone.

Chayele grinned as Ruth joined them. "Isn't this amazing? Half of New York City is here."

Ruth chuckled at Chayele's exaggeration, but she did marvel at the turnout—far bigger than expected. "Clara still wouldn't give them another chance?"

Chayele shook her head. "She said despite the cause she couldn't align herself with the elitist Mink Brigade on principle."

Anne spoke from behind them. "All right, ladies I have room for one more person to sit in the car. The others will follow along."

Chayele grinned and took a step to the car.

"Oh wait. Ruth! I didn't see you there." Anne smiled and waved her over. "Ruth, come ride with us. You need to meet everyone."

Ruth took a hesitant step forward as Chayele scowled at the slight. Ignoring her, Anne stepped forward and slipped an arm around Ruth's shoulders.

"I've told them all about you," Anne said. She looked back over her shoulder at the others. "Thank you, girls, for supporting us by marching. We'll see you all at the end."

Ruth looked away uncomfortably from Chayele's glare and tried to focus on what Anne was saying. As she settled into the car, she glanced out the window and saw Ester pushing through the crowd. Her heart leapt in excitement as she imagined her sister changing her mind and coming to join the parade.

But then Ester stopped as someone caught her arm and pulled her back. Abraham appeared next to her, and Ruth watched as he took the marketing basket from Ester's hand and held it for her. Ester tilted her head back and laughed at something he said, and he smiled. Ruth frowned as she realized the tired, pained expression he'd worn this morning was now gone. She watched him take Ester's arm and steer her back through the crowd, away from the car where Ruth sat. Ruth sorted through a flood of confused feelings as the car moved forward. She was glad Ester was there for him when he needed someone. But when was the last time either of them had laughed or smiled with *her*?

"Ruth? Have you met Mrs. Schar yet?"

Ruth looked up as Anne interrupted her thoughts.

"She's fascinated by your story," Anne gushed.

"No, I haven't." Ruth leaned forward to join the conversation. She'd think about Ester and Abraham later. She'd find a way to make it up to them. They couldn't stay angry forever.

Abraham

Saturday October 9th, 1910

165 Days Until the Fire

Abraham stepped inside and was immediately bumped by a laughing couple with sloshing cups of ale. The man stopped to apologize before slinging his arm around the woman and leading her away. Abraham brushed off his wet sleeve and grumbled to himself. This was a mistake. He wasn't in the mood, and he hated these crowded saloons, anyway.

But Yankel had insisted. "You need to blow off some steam! Enjoy your freedom while you still can!"

Abraham didn't care about what Yankel called

freedom. But he did give in when Yankel accused him of standoffishness. Abraham felt guilty for being less available to his friend since Ruth's arrival. They just lived such different lives now.

Using his height to his advantage, he scanned the crowded room. He spotted Yankel leaning on the bar in the back, chatting with a cute blonde girl. Definitely not Jewish. *So much for male bonding.* Abraham tried to quell his irritation as he pushed through the crowd to them. He didn't want to start the evening being annoyed. After all, Yankel had been there for him so many times—including that night last spring, when Abraham had stormed out on Ruth.

He finally broke through the crowd and sidled up to join Yankel at the bar. Yankel raised his eyebrows to acknowledge Abraham and continued his conversation with the girl, while Abraham busied himself with catching the bartender's eye. By the time the drink was in front of him, Yankel had ditched the girl and joined him with his own half-empty glass.

"Abe, you made it!"

Abraham took a sip. "I said I would."

"How does it feel being out of your cell?"

Abraham rolled his eyes.

Yankel laughed. "I've been surveying my prospects. That blonde is a possibility. A little *yutzi*"—he tapped above his ear— "Not too much up there, but eh?" He shrugged.

Abraham shook his head. "Don't you get tired of *schmoozing* different girls all the time? How do you have the energy? They last what, a month at most?"

Yankel took a sip of ale. "What's the alternative? Being stuck like you? Committed to an awful shrew who ignores me?"

Abraham took a deep breath. He wanted to snap at Yankel, but again remembered his rant that one night. Was that really how he'd portrayed Ruth?

"That's not fair. Ruth's not awful."

Yankel surveyed his glass and fingered a bead of condensation. "But she *is* a shrew who ignores you?"

"She's got a lot of *chutzpah* and can be single-minded, ya, but she's passionate."

Yankel leaned closer. "You do realize there are other options? Just look at the beauties in this room."

Abraham laughed. "Many of whom are equally opinionated and even more Americanized."

"There are plenty of traditional women if that's what you want."

Abraham waved his hand. "Not here, there's not."

Yankel smiled. "Maybe not at this saloon. But tucked away home in their beds, so they can be up cooking tomorrow."

A momentary image of Ester flashed through his head. Abraham closed his eyes at the thought. "I already know the 'perfect traditional girl'."

Yankel nudged him. "Then what's keeping you? Are you that scared of your father or hers? Is it your guilt over your friend? What?"

Why wouldn't he drop it? Abraham bristled in frustration at Yankel's persistence. He wasn't scared of the fathers. Sure, they meddled and tried to dictate authority. But when it came down to it, they knew they had none—not here in America. If he really wanted out of the betrothal, they wouldn't stop him. It would be awkward with their families so intertwined, but even that wasn't what was really keeping him.

The guilt over his promise to Jeremiah—ya, that had mattered in the beginning. But did it now? His gut clenched as he realized he'd barely even thought of Jeremiah recently. It was like the tension weighing down on him had finally been released after sharing what had happened back in Russia.

So, why *was* he still committed to Ruth, when they did nothing but argue and she prioritized all her causes over him? Why, when he could see how much easier life could be with someone like Ester?

Memories and images flooded his head. Ruth's wide-eyed wonder as she watched the movie for the first time. Her screeching with joy on the Gravity Switchback rollercoaster at Luna Park. The two of them, laughing as they shared a slice of watermelon on Orchard Street, competing to see who could spit their seed the furthest. And his whole body glowed with warmth when he remembered her kisses—though there hadn't been many of those yet.

He ducked his head. "It's her," he mumbled.

"What?" Yankel asked.

"*She's* keeping me. I love *her.*"

Yankel laughed. "Oh, you are in trouble!"

Abraham fiddled with the glass in front of him. "There's just a spark. Something there. I don't know."

"You really don't think it'd be easier to start over with someone else? Recreate the spark?" Yankel asked.

Abraham shook his head. "I'd just compare them to her. She's one of a kind."

"Love," Yankel scoffed. He picked up his glass and drained it. "Makes us miserable and yet we can't live without it." His empty glass clanked on the bar-top. "Which is why I'm still searching for my own misery-invoking spark."

He clapped a hand on Abraham's shoulder and squeezed. Then he turned away to return to the crowd. Abraham watched as he rejoined the blonde girl. He leaned down and whispered something in her ear. The girl tossed her head back and laughed.

It would be easy to start from scratch with someone new. A clean slate without resentments and hurt feelings. But then, wouldn't the same thing happen again? Didn't any relationship eventually build up to conflict in some form?

He thought back to his parents when they were together in Russia. He remembered the shared loving looks and gestures. His father putting his hand at the small of his mother's back when he came up behind her while she was washing dishes. How she'd bring him a cup of tea while he read Scripture at the kitchen table and drop a kiss on his head. But there were also the nights he heard things he wasn't supposed to. Whispered angry voices. The slam of a door. No, his parents' relationship hadn't been perfect either.

Maybe that was the secret. No relationship would ever be perfect. Yankel could continue searching for something shiny and new, but Abraham had a foundation with Ruth. Something he was starting to build. And ya, here in America he had a choice in who he married. He could continue searching for something better, if it even existed. Or he could learn from his parents and *choose* to stay. Repair the cracks in the foundation and try to make it stronger.

He glanced over to where Yankel was cozied up with the blonde. He was telling a story and gesturing wildly with his hands. The blonde girl put her hand on his arm and said something that made him grin.

Ah, it would be easy. He could walk over there right now to join them. He could chat up one of the blonde's friends and have a girl look at him that way, listening with eyes wide and putting her hand on *his* arm. When was the last time Ruth had done that?

He watched for another moment and then shook his head. He chugged the last of his ale and slammed the glass back onto the bar. It was time to go home.

As he pushed back through the crowd to the door, he felt a tingle of excitement rush through him. He paused to look back over the busy saloon—everyone leaning in and shouting to be heard. Drinks sloshing and people stumbling. He smiled to himself and walked out the door. He couldn't wait to get home to Ruth.

E s t e r

December 16th, 1910

99 Days Until the Fire

A few lone snowflakes fell from the sky as Ester trudged home from work. Ahead of her, the other girls walked arm in arm. Ruth was talking, waving her hands in that animated way she had. Behind, she heard the low murmur of Abraham and Yankel's voices. As usual, she was with them—but not really "with them." Normally, Ester didn't mind this much because she would have her own social time later when she went to her night class at the Teacher's College. But it was Friday and they didn't have class on Fridays. At least, she'd get home in time to help Momme finish the Shabbat preparations.

A change in the girls' body language ahead caught her eye. They were all hunched over and leaning into each other. Their voices had also dropped lower. What were they discussing so secretively?

"Oy, Chayele!" Yankel shouted from behind Ester, making her jump. "This is our block!"

Yankel and Chayele separated from the group and everyone else said their goodbyes and went their own ways as well. Abraham turned to Ester and Ruth.

"Will you be alright from here?" Abraham was joining Tatty and Samuel for the *haftarah* reading at synagogue for *Hannukah*.

Ester nodded. He gave Ruth's arm a squeeze and took off towards Eldridge Street.

"What were you all talking about?"

Ruth tossed her hair. "Oh, you know, the usual. Work, hair, weekend plans."

Ester gave Ruth a sharp look. "That doesn't require whispers. What are you up to?"

Ruth ignored her and kept walking. Ester stood in place. "I'm not moving until you tell me! And you know I mean it!"

Ruth stopped and turned back to face Ester.

People brushed past them as the two girls held their ground, each waiting for the other to give in. Finally, Ruth let out a growling sigh and stalked back to her. Ester had to stop herself from breaking into a grin.

"Why do you have to be so childish?" Ruth grumbled. She pulled Ester along as she spoke. "Clara is launching a new branch of the women's suffrage league called the Wage Earners' League."

Ester pulled away. "What does that mean?"

"It means they will focus on the needs of working women, not the needs of the rich."

Ester felt a knot growing in her stomach. "Why does this concern you? You've given that up, haven't you?"

Ruth looked away and Ester felt heat flood her face. How could she have been so stupid? Of course, Ruth hadn't just been going to meet her friends for "chats" at Mirele and Zusa's, or English lessons with Filomena! She'd been meeting to plot next moves.

"Are you still working with that *shiksa* woman?"

"Anne has been very good to me. I'm feeling very disloyal about leaving her to join Clara."

Ester bit back a feeling of rage. "What about loyalty to family? To Abraham who believes you're done with marches and protests?"

"Abraham's not stupid! He knows I've still been attending suffragette meetings."

Ester nodded slowly. "All right. Perhaps. But there's a big difference in handing out pamphlets and marching in parades with Anne and the suffragettes. How will Clara lead things? You know her, Ruth. She's a radical, an agitator. There will be strikes and who knows what! What will she expect of you?"

Ruth shrugged. "I don't know yet. Tonight is the first meeting."

Ester felt her jaw drop. "But tonight is *Shabbat*. And it's the last night of *Hannukah.*"

Ruth didn't answer. Which was an answer in itself. She didn't care. How could Ruth give up her family and heritage so easily? What was it about Clara and these women that captivated her so?

Ester knew what it was like be caught up in a movement. Her involvement with Hedy and the Jewish Education Bureau had shown her how good it felt to be part of something bigger and better than yourself. She understood that, she did. But she also felt closer to her family after each of her meetings. She could see how each proposed item on the Bureau's agenda, each improvement they were fighting for, would *benefit* the family. Whereas with Ruth, it was the opposite. The deeper she got, the more her activities pulled her away. Why couldn't her sister see that?

They turned onto Orchard Street, and Ruth fumbled at her pocket. She pulled out a list with Momme's curvy scrawl. "I promised Momme we'd pick up a few things on our way home." As Ruth read, Ester took in the busy marketplace. She soaked in the comforting sounds of the heavily accented voices rising and falling in Yiddish. The familiar sights and smells of Jewish culture.

Ester watched as Ruth pushed her way to the front of a gaggle of people by the apple cart, picked up the last few shiny red apples and began to haggle with the vendor, ignoring the crowd at her back.

She remembered Ruth haggling like that back in St. Petersburg, getting as much bruised and beaten produce as possible for what meager sum of money they possessed. Ruth had grown up doing this, and did it well, always managing to keep food on the table.

Ester watched as the apple-cart vendor finally waved her hand in defeat. Ruth dropped a few coins into the woman's hand and turned back to Ester with a triumphant smile. Ruth complained so much about the intricacies of Jewish cooking and home life. Yet how could she not see how much she belonged to her culture?

Together, they navigated the crowded marketplace to get the last two items on Momme's list before climbing the stairs back to their building.

As they neared the first landing, Ester asked. "What are you going to tell Momme and Tatty?"

"I was hoping you'd cover me. Tell them I had to go because Zusa was sick."

"Why couldn't Mirele take care of her?"

"You got something better?" Ruth chewed her lip.

Ester sighed. "I hate lying. Why must you go tonight? Can't you enjoy the last night of *Hannukah* with us and have Chayele fill you in tomorrow?"

Ruth rubbed her temples. "They need me. They're building their entire premise tonight. Their board, goals and directions, all of it."

Ester suddenly understood. "This isn't about them needing you. You want this. So you can feel in charge."

Ester turned away from Ruth and continued up the last flight of stairs to their apartment. The insensitivity of Clara even holding such a meeting on a Friday night— and during *Hannukah* no less! This was exactly what she and Hedy were working against. These American Jews giving up their culture and beliefs and dragging others down with them!

She turned back to say so to Ruth, but Ruth was gone. The bag of apples sat at the bottom of the stairs. Her fury sprang to life. How dare Ruth! The coward had actually left Ester not only to cover and lie for her, but to do it alone. She stomped down and grabbed the bag of apples. She craned her neck, but sure enough, there was no sign of Ruth. Just neighbors chatting in the hallway by the front door. She sighed and trudged up the stairs.

Opening the door, she found Momme in a flurry of preparations. The kitchen was a mess and the table still wasn't set. The baby wailed in the cradle and something was burning on the stove.

"Where's Ruth?"

Ester wrung her hands. "Uhm, she's not coming. She got called away…"

Momme paused with a puzzled frown for a moment before hurrying to grab the burning pan from the stove.

✳ ✳ ✳

Ester set the last plate on the table and reached to turn a serving bowl so its handle faced Tatty.

Momme spoke from the chair where she sat nursing the baby. "It's perfect, *sheifale.* Thank you."

The door opened. The men had returned from synagogue. Tatty smiled and patted his stomach. "Ah, smells delicious!"

They hung their coats and hats. Abraham scanned the apartment. "Where's Ruth?"

Momme stiffened and looked up from the baby. "She left us for the evening."

Ester's neck grew hot as she spoke. "Mirele sent word that Zusa had fallen ill and she needed Ruth's help to care for her."

Momme exchanged a look with Tatty. Abraham clenched his hand into a fist by his side. Ester could see him hardening his jaw.

"Mirele couldn't care for Zusa on her own? Why does she need Ruth?" Tatty finally asked.

Ester twisted a dishcloth in her hands. Why did Ruth leave her to tell these lies on her own? "Uhm, I guess she felt Ruth had more experience— you know, caring for me back in Russia?"

Momme stood and placed the now sleeping baby back in the cradle. She buttoned up her dress and gestured to the *menorah*. "Well, let's light the candles before the sun goes down." She patted Tatty on the shoulder as he picked up the box of matches. He caught her hand and gave it a squeeze.

They said their prayers as they lit the *menorah*. Then they sat at the table and passed the plates of heaping food. Although everything was delicious as usual, the banter and conversation felt forced. Ester caught everyone darting uneasy glances at Ruth's empty chair. When Tatty and Samuel finally leaned back to loosen their pants, Momme jumped to her feet to gather dishes as if she couldn't wait to escape.

Ester started to help Momme, but Abraham grabbed her arm and pulled her to the parlor.

"Where is she really?" he asked.

Ester's stomach rolled. She tried to avoid his searching gaze.

"Come on, Ester. We both know she's not nursing a sick Zusa. That girl was practically skipping home from work today."

She looked up to face him and saw the desperation in his eyes. How could she lie to him? To Abraham, who was the most honest, good person she knew? Didn't he deserve more than that?

She wet her lips. Her voice shook as she spoke. "She went to a meeting with Clara and Chayele. Clara is creating a new Wage Earners Suffragette League. They're formalizing the charter and board tonight."

Abraham sucked in his breath. "And Ruth will

be a part of this? The founding of this new league?"

Ester nodded. She watched as something shattered within him. His shoulders slumped and his eyes darkened.

Ester reached for him, but he turned away. There was nothing more she could do. Ruth didn't deserve a man so loyal and loving. The unfairness of it all raged within her.

If only…

R u t h

Friday March 24th, 1911

1 Day Until the Fire

Ruth reveled in the peaceful setting, the March sunlight dancing on the water and a seagull swooping down and squawking, adding its voice to the chatter as people gathered at the Ellis Island arrivals gate. Ruth's mind wandered as Tatty led the family in prayer while they waited for Abraham's family. *"Blessed are you, Hashem, our God, King of the Universe, the Good and the Doer of good, for reuniting us today."* Ruth glanced at Abraham to try and gauge his feelings. Was he nervous to see his family again? But his gaze remained fixed on the ground before him.

Samuel burst forward, waving and shouting in Yiddish, as Abraham's mother, Sarah, pushed her way through the crowd. They jumped into each other's arms. The children found Abraham and wrapped their arms around his waist.

"Benyamin, Calev—you boys are huge," Abraham laughed. "And Leah, you were just a toddler when I last saw you!" Ruth could see the emotions clouding his eyes. He clutched his three siblings as if squeezing them tight could bring back the years.

Sarah finally broke away from Samuel and found Momme standing on the outskirts of the reunion. She gathered Momme into a tight hug, dislodging Momme's careful bun while her own shawl flapped in the breeze.

Samuel and Tatty chuckled, "The hens are finally reunited."

✳ ✳ ✳

The small Orchard Street apartment echoed with laughter and chatter that evening. Momme tried to create more room for the ten people at the table with a makeshift addition of overturned milk crates covered by sheets. But no one seemed to mind being squished together. Momme, Ruth and Ester had spent the week cooking, and in addition to the wine and *challah*, the table was filled with traditional favorites from home and a mix of new "American" treats dropped off by some of their non-Jewish, well-wishing neighbors.

Amid the happy sounds, Tatty pushed his chair back and stood with a raised glass. "I feel blessed to have all of us honor *Shabbat* under one roof again. Samuel and I have long said that we are really one extended family. Which we can't wait to make official at the wedding this weekend." He grinned and looked to Ruth and Abraham. "So now that Samuel's family has finally made the journey here to America, my family is also complete again. *L'chaim!"*

"L'chaim," they echoed and glasses clinked.

"We don't need to take that 'one roof' statement literally, do we? We're looking forward to a bit more space of our own," Samuel joked.

Tatty chuckled. "I suppose the same building or the one next door would work. But no farther! I will not allow it!"

He patted Samuel on the back and they got up to find more wine.

Sarah leaned over and cooed at the new baby girl in Momme's arms. As they laughed, their eyes filled up again. There were lines on Sarah's face that Ruth had never seen. What had Sarah experienced in Russia? Had she lied in her letters, just as Ruth and Momme had lied when they wrote to Tatty and Abraham during that seemingly endless final winter in Moscow—when Ester was sick and they had scraped up every grain of wheat from the bottom of the barrel? Momme had scrutinized every letter Ruth wrote as carefully as one of the czar's censors. *Don't say anything negative. What's the point of worrying them?*

As the meal went on, Ruth saw flashes of understanding between the two best friends. There would be time to catch up on everything now. Time, at last, for them to unload their burdens, each to the other.

Ruth surveyed the scene around the rest of the table. Ester sat alone, keeping herself apart from everyone. She wore a blank expression, betraying no thoughts or emotions—as usual. Ester never said anything hurtful directly, but she always seemed distant, and she disappeared every night without explanation. Ruth hoped her sister had a new beau, but Ester clammed up and got angry when Ruth asked. So, Ruth left her alone now, the gap between them growing ever wider. Would she be able to repair these relationships she'd once treasured more than anything?

Next to Ester, Abraham's brothers played a game where they hit each other across the knuckles with their silverware. Abraham sat next to them, smiling at every movement and laugh.

He was smiling. *Really* smiling, with his eyes, for practically the first time in months. She barely recognized him, this man who was laughing and joking with his brothers. Like the boy she had grown up with. The Abraham she had played cards with in her parlor in Russia and had thought was gone forever. Here he was. He only needed his family to bring that side of him to the surface. Could he ever again behave that way with her?

She would find a way.

Ruth felt a weight lift from her shoulders. Maybe they could hope for a better future. She saw him lift his eyes—had he felt her gaze? —and offer a shy smile. She felt a flicker of excitement and smiled back.

An hour later Ruth stood at the sink drying dishes.

"Want to go for a walk?" Abraham whispered.

Ruth blushed. The kids were collapsed in heaps around the room and the married adults were gathered around the table with another bottle of wine. Momme and Sarah were discussing the wedding menu. It was the perfect opportunity to escape, and she was pleased he'd offered. She turned around to face him. Tilting her chin up, he brushed a stray curl away from her eyes. She took his hand and led him to the front door, where he grabbed her coat and held it out for her. She shivered, remembering their first walk together. Her first day in America. The day he'd proposed. That day had held such optimism. She'd been naïve, underestimating how hard the next two years would be. But perhaps there was still hope for them.

Ruth looked over at Abraham as they began their descent to the street. He appeared to be lost in thought, but met her gaze with a small smile before reaching over to take her hand. As they neared the second-floor landing, one of the gas lamps flickered and went dark. Abraham cursed under his breath before squeezing Ruth's hand in reassurance.

"Here, lean on me so we can navigate together."

It felt like the minutes and steps crawled by until finally her foot made contact with the flat entranceway floor. She exhaled a huge sigh as they sped through the dimly lit hall to the outside.

Abraham chuckled when they stepped outside. "Well, hope you were planning on staying out a while. Because the real adventure will be going back up."

She groaned. "That landlord is useless."

Abraham shrugged and withdrew his hand to adjust his hat. It was a clear night with only a slight chill in the air. With darkness having already descended, most people were already home observing *Shabbat*. The marketplace was deserted except for one lone pushcart. A few other couples strolled leisurely in the street, enjoying the first glimpse of spring. Abraham and Ruth walked in silence for a bit before she cleared her throat.

"It must be overwhelming to see your family again."

He cracked a half-smile. "A bit. But satisfying as well. It's amazing to see how much they've all grown."

She chewed her lip. "I'm sorry Devorah isn't here.

She knew his sister's decision to stay in Russia upset him.

"I understand why she chose to stay. She's built a life. I just wish I could have seen her get married."

"Your mother said he's a lovely man."

"They'll be happy. God-willing," he said.

They fell silent again and Ruth wondered what to say next. That had been the first real conversation they'd had in months. But before she could think any further, he spoke again.

"What do you think our life would have been

like if I'd stayed?"

"Our life?" she echoed.

"Well, our fathers were already negotiating our betrothal. So, it stands to reason we would have been married that year."

Yes, she'd thought about it—for example, that day she'd watched her parents dance in the apartment. But for some reason, she never thought Abraham might be imagining the same thing.

"I suppose you're right," she said slowly. "We'd have been married and perhaps even have a few children by now."

He smiled at her words. "How different things would have been if I'd never left. If I'd been there to protect you, you wouldn't have needed to work in the factory or worry about providing for everyone."

Her breath caught. "Are you saying *I* would have been different?"

"I don't know. I'd like to blame America for our problems. But I think it does go back to you being left behind."

"Because I learned to take care of myself?"

She noticed they were actually speaking to each other without anger or resentment. For the first time, they were being completely honest with each other.

He shivered slightly. "It's not that I mind you being

able to take care of yourself."

"Oh, thank God, you don't mind," she broke in.

He scowled and she stopped. Keep the conversation civil, she reminded herself.

He took a deep breath. "Try to understand. I'm fine with you being able to take care of yourself. I admire that. I've told you before, your strength is one of my favorite things about you."

Surprised, she tilted her head. "Then why have you been so angry?"

"Because it's like you have something to prove." His voice rose. "Like you *alone* can take care of everyone."

"I don't understand. You're angry because I care about others?"

Visibly frustrated, he dragged his hand through his hair. "The girls and Clara's union meetings, the suffragettes. You have nothing left for us."

"That's not true! I care for you all."

"How exactly, Ruth? When you ignored your father about *Shabbat*? Or when you brushed aside my feelings about Blanck?"

"That's not fair." She crossed her arms. "You wanted me to sacrifice my beliefs to squelch your fears."

"And after everything we'd been through, that was

too much to ask? You needed to make us worry and suffer more?"

"Well, if you want to argue that, it was you who made us all suffer the first time around. Why should I be held back because you got our brothers killed?"

He cringed.

Horrified at how that came out, she held up her hands. "I'm sorry. I didn't mean that." Her voice softened. "What I mean is, why does it always have to be a choice?"

"Because our lives don't work that way, Ruth."

His voice was tight, and she realized how much she'd wounded him. He might never forget what she'd said about their brothers. But she couldn't unsay it.

She should be kinder, she knew. It's not that she didn't believe what she said. But why could she never hold back? Why couldn't she govern her tongue, abide until the right moment? Part of her hated him for making her despise herself.

Tears came to her eyes. "Because you want me being a good *berryer*?" she heard herself say. "Making sure dinner is ready when you get home?" She couldn't stop the words spilling from her mouth.

He frowned and shook his head. "No, because I can't sit on the side feeling like I don't matter."

She reeled at his words. "You think you don't

matter?" Her voice cracked. "Of course, you matter."

"Then why do you choose everyone and everything over me? The fights will never end. There are dozens of Max Blancks out there. You can't defeat them all."

"I have to try!" she cried. "You've just given up! I can't close my eyes like you."

"So, what, you're just going to bring our future children to the picket line and suffragette parades?" he mocked. "Teach them to write by making signs? Is that the life you see for us?"

"Of course not," she sniffed.

"Well, what then? How do you plan to balance this life?"

She flailed her hands. "I don't know!"

He whispered, "Because you know it's impossible."

He turned and stalked away, heading back home.

Ruth watched helplessly. Was he really going to leave her here on the dark street alone?

He hesitated a moment and Ruth took a step forward, her mind fumbling for what she should say when he turned around.

But he clenched his fists and continued to walk. Ruth's stomach fell as she stared after his fading shape.

R u t h

Ruth sighed as she ripped out another stitch. That was the fifth mistake she'd made today.

Ester frowned. "You're spending more time correcting stitches than making new ones. We won't make quota."

"Quit fussing," Ruth snapped. She looked over her shoulder to see if anyone had overheard.

Heads were down, the women focused on work. She could hear nothing from the other tables over the growl of the machines. Next to her, Chayele winked.

"No one but us to hear you two pecking at each other. But make speed, I've got a date picking me up at five sharp and I don't intend to keep him waiting. And you, Ruth—you've got to get your rest so you look beautiful for your wedding tomorrow! Then you'll be busy darning your husband's socks while we're all slaving away here."

Ruth didn't reply. For some reason, she didn't like to be teased about the wedding, though she knew it was the normal thing.

She tried to work faster. Their whole table seemed to be slow today. Other than Ester and Chayele, the others weren't up to their usual speed. Mirele and Zusa had been in gossip mode all day, discussing a problem with one of their roommates, and Filomena was nursing a bad head cold. She sneezed loudly from the other end of the table and wiped her nose on her sleeve.

Ruth bent her head in an attempt to focus, but movement from across the room caught her attention. Mr. Blanck's daughters and their governess were arriving to meet him for a Saturday shopping trip.

She scowled as the girls sauntered across the workroom with an air of entitlement, wearing their pretty coats, buttoned-up ankle boots, and muffs. Mr. Blanck met them at the door and craned his neck to check on the progress at the workstations. He caught Ruth's eye and frowned at her idleness. As he turned to his daughters, she stuck out her tongue at the back of his head.

Ruth shoved the shirt sleeve back into her machine. She rushed through the stitches and grabbed the next shirt sleeve from the pile as she glanced at the clock on the wall. 4:30. Only half an hour left. By this time tomorrow, she'd be married. Life as she knew it would change forever. She would never be coming back to this factory again, except maybe to meet Abraham and walk home with him. Maybe that was why she was having such difficulty focusing; a part of her almost wanted to savor these last thirty minutes. She shook her head to focus and pumped her foot harder as she fed another shirt into the machine.

"Ouch." She stuck her pricked finger in her mouth and sucked on the drop of blood quickly forming there.

"Here, give me that." Ester grabbed the sleeve from Ruth's hand. "Do you want us owing money by the end of the shift?"

"Who made you boss?" Ruth grumbled, but she let Ester fix the sleeve for her.

From across the room, Abraham caught her eye. Since his promotion to collar and union leader, he'd been rewarded with a position next to the windows that provided welcome air to offset the hot machines. The late afternoon March sunlight shone in from the window, highlighting the streaks of blond in his chestnut hair. A small smile played on her lips. Despite all their issues, she still found him incredibly handsome. His blue shirt was rumpled, though, and his face was pale with dark circles under his eyes. He must have had trouble sleeping, as she did after their fight last night. He didn't smile back—just looked back down to his machine.

"He's still mad at me," Ruth said. "What can I do?"

"You'll be married tomorrow. You'll sort it out." Ester picked up another shirt sleeve off Ruth's pile. Ruth swatted her hand away.

"Focus on your pile. I can do my own work, thanks."

"But I'm already finished."

Ruth looked at Ester's empty pile and her own diminished stack. Ester had somehow managed to knock off five shirtsleeves in two minutes. She couldn't help but marvel—her younger sister had found her calling. She gave her finger one last suck and fed another shirtsleeve into the machine.

"You didn't answer me. What should I do about Abraham?"

Ester didn't reply. She looked away from Ruth's expectant gaze as she fed a shirtsleeve into the machine. Her cheeks flushed.

"I don't know what you want," she finally said. "You pushed us all away doing exactly what you wanted. You had to know there'd be consequences."

"But I wasn't doing it for *me*."

"So you've said. But why did it matter so much, Ruth? Why did it matter *so much*?"

Ruth shrugged. "I'm quitting work to be his wife. He knows he's my priority." She reached for a shirtsleeve, but Ester caught her hand.

Ester's gaze seemed to search Ruth's face. She almost looked desperate—though why would she be? "Is he what you really want?"

Ruth opened her mouth to answer, but screams erupted from the kindergarten corner behind them. They turned to look and froze, motionless. The conversation, which had seemed so urgent, vanished from Ruth's mind in an instant.

Licks of flames were spilling from the air shaft.

Ruth slowly rose from her seat. Her mind struggled to take in what she was seeing. Fire? Here? In the factory? Why wasn't anyone putting it out?

She watched, stunned, as the factory transformed within seconds. Tendrils of smoke billowed up the walls and filled the air. Ruth started coughing. Suddenly, all around her, she heard coughs, then shrieks. Only a minute before—less than a minute— it had been a dull, ordinary afternoon. Now girls leapt from their seats. Ruth stared disbelieving at the dancing flames.

Until Ester grabbed her arm and *pulled*.

The aisles—there were only three, and too narrow for such an onslaught—were quickly filled with frantic workers. Panicked girls tried to scramble over the tops of the machines while others tried crawling underneath them. Ruth watched in horror as the girls' skirts caught on the heavy machine parts, trapping them. They screamed in terror as the flames leapt closer.

Ester yanked Ruth into the single-file line pushing to the right aisle. Over her shoulder, Ruth glimpsed Chayele and the other girls close behind. But she lost sight of them as Ester elbowed her nearer the Greene Street staircase—the closest exit, but there was a backup of almost a hundred people, crying and trying to push their way down.

Ester yanked Ruth away. "Come on! Let's try the other side." They hiked up their skirts and climbed atop the machines.

"Do you see Abraham?" Ruth screamed at Ester.

Ester shook her head. "I'm sure he's ahead though."

They skittered to the end of the row of machines and hopped down, nearly knocking over the people mobbing the left-hand aisle.

"We'll find him, don't worry." Ester squeezed Ruth's hand as they joined the mass seething toward the Washington Street staircase.

They were only a few feet from the exit when they heard shouts ahead. The crowd stopped abruptly.

"It's locked, damn it!" a man's voice thundered.

Ruth heard booming noises—fists slamming the door.

Another voice called, "Let me try." Then, "It won't budge!"

"Where's the key?"

"Where's Grosevich?"

"The coward took off already!"

The room grew hotter by the second. Everywhere

Ruth looked, she saw fire. The scrap heaps and piles on the work stations, and the baskets of fabric underneath the tables, were consumed with flames. Ruth's chest tightened and her eyes watered from the smoke. She covered her mouth with her sleeve.

"The elevator," she wheezed.

They turned to push against the crowd. Glass broke in the distance. Ruth vaguely remembered Mr. Blanck bragging to Abraham about the state-of-the art fire safety precautions he'd installed. A bucket went flying over her head and hit the wall. Some of the men must be trying to put the fire out

"The hose is empty!" someone cursed.

The blanket of smoke thickened and settled over the room, and the shoving grew rougher. Ruth clutched Ester's hand, drawing blood with her fingernails as they rode the tidal wave of bodies pushing to the elevators. She cringed to hear screaming—people being burned or trampled. Then she felt the soft cushion of body parts under her own feet, but she was trapped in the surge and couldn't break away or stop. The elevator doors towered like a beacon ahead. The last chance for escape. She heard the faint ding as Joseph's elevator arrived and the doors opened. The crowd pressed forward and, still clutching Ester's hand, she was thrown into the car.

"Stop! Stop! There's too many!" Joseph screamed. "The elevator can't hold everyone."

Someone yanked Ruth's hair from behind and kicked her knees as people fought for her spot. The elevator swayed from the weight. The crowd ebbed and flowed like violent waves crashing and tearing away from shore, as people continued to shove their way on, meeting equal force by the elevator passengers pushing back.

"Hold on, everyone. We have to go!" Joseph yelled. "Gaspar will be right back for another trip. Step back!" He pulled on the chain link door. Passengers in the car grabbed hold to help him. From the other side, panicked people tried to pull the other way. Just as the door was about to close, Ester suddenly released Ruth's hand and shimmied through the half inch of space out of the elevator.

"What are you doing?" Ruth screamed.

"I'm sorry, Ruth!" Ester sobbed. "I'm sorry!"

The elevator door closed and Joseph slammed the lever. The elevator jerked and dropped downward.

E s t e r

Saturday March 25ᵗʰ, 1911

The Day of the Fire

A cacophony of sounds surrounded and suffocated her. Ruth's screams as the elevator doors clanked shut. The whir of the contraption springing to life, then dropping.

Ester steeled herself to push against the crowd, to get away. Her feet stumbled across something squishy—or someone. She felt herself almost go down and inhaled sharply, praying she would not become one of those trampled bodies. Luckily, she was so crammed in from every side, she was able to regain her balance by bouncing off the person next to her.

She was crazy. She'd been in the elevator on her way to safety. But she'd changed her mind when she saw the flash of blue.

Abraham's shirt.

She'd know it anywhere. It was she who had bought the fabric at the marketplace—spent a whole week's wages on it, painstakingly stitched the seams when everyone else was asleep. It was overstepping to give him such a gift, but she hadn't been able to resist. It was the same color as his eyes.

She pushed against the tide of panicked workers, Ruth's screams still echoing in her mind. But Ruth was safe, Ester reminded herself. She'd seen Joseph wrap her in his strong, comforting arms as the elevator lurched down. Ruth would get outside and Ester would rejoin her soon enough. With Abraham in tow.

Ester snaked her way through the crowd, back to the wall of machines. The fire had now overtaken the back half of the room.

She spotted the blue again by the window and lunged for it. She bobbed and weaved her way around panicked girls rushing from the flames and snatched at it before it disappeared.

"Abraham!"

"Ester! *Hashem yishmor!*" He gripped her arms. "I've been searching. Where's Ruth?"

She gestured to the elevators. "I got her to safety."

His eyebrows rose in a puzzled expression. "You didn't go?"

"Not without you. You know—you know I'd do anything—." She was amazed to hear her own words. They'd sprung from her without any conscious planning. Somehow, because of the danger, because of the fire, she was saying things she'd never allowed herself to say.

She searched his face for any sign of his feelings. His eyes were cloudy and his jaw was tight. She groped for his hand, but he drew back.

For a moment she was stunned, and then her insides crumbled. He loved Ruth, even after everything. There was no time, now, to continue the conversation—in whatever way it could continue. He had destroyed all her hopes.

She was distracted by a screech of metal as the chain-link elevator door was pried open.

A crowd pressed to the open shaft and then there was a blood-curdling scream.

"People are jumping—jumping down the shaft!"

Ester cringed and looked away. The heat suddenly

felt overpowering. The fire had gained in strength in even the few minutes she and Abraham had been speaking. The path between them and the elevator and stairways was now overtaken by orange flames. Girls huddled together crying, clutching handkerchiefs to their faces and climbing chairs and machinery to try and escape. A girl shrieked as her skirt caught fire and two others attempted to help her put it out.

Ester looked to Abraham. "We're not getting out, are we?"

He surveyed the room. She could almost see the shifting wheels in his head. His jaw clenched in grim determination.

"Come." He turned for the window behind them.

She gasped as he slid it open and she understood his plan. He offered her his hand.

She took one last glance around the room—all the faces, all the combinations of desperation, despair, and resignation. She knew they had no choice. She took his outstretched hand and they clambered onto the windowsill. Ester observed the scene nine stories below. Desperate firefighters running to and from, propping ladders up against the building. But the ladders didn't reach nearly high enough.

"Look!" Abraham said. "They have nets!"

Hope fluttered in Ester's stomach at the sight of the unfolding nets. She mentally calculated the odds—they'd have to land directly in the center. The firefighters would have to hold on, even with the force of both their weights. It was desperate. But it was possible.

Abraham squeezed her hand and she turned to him.

He leaned to her and cupped her face gently. "Thank you for coming back for me."

She closed her eyes as his lips met her cheek. His lips were soft and warm.

He slowly pulled away. She opened her eyes as he brushed her hair with his finger. "Ready on three?"

She nodded. He squeezed her hand one more time and began to count. He got to three.

She closed her eyes and jumped.

Ruth

"No!"

Ruth beat the chain link door with both her hands, then clawed at it, trying to rip it open. But the chain rattled and clanked, and the elevator went down.

"We have to go back," she begged. "We have to!"

Someone slammed her from behind and her knees buckled. But she continued pulling at the door.

"Stop her!" a voice growled. "She's gonna kill us."

Joseph dragged her away from the door. Ruth collapsed against his chest and saw blood—her blood? —where her fingers gripped his white shirt.

"I'll go back," he soothed. "I'll get her, I promise."

Clank.

Joseph pushed her into the corner and returned to the controls.

Clank.

"Is that the other elevator?" a woman gulped.

Thump.

The roof dented and plaster cracked from the ceiling. The elevator lurched, and a pervading smell of smoke and singed flesh invaded the car. Gasping, the passengers ducked and huddled. There were muffled bangs and choked sobs.

Ruth stared helplessly at soot-smeared fingerprints on the elevator wall. More and more thumps came. The elevator creaked and groaned. Then *snap*—it fell.

Limbs and elbows crashed together. Ruth clutched the people around her—whatever she could grab—as her feet lost contact with the floor. Her stomach dropped as she flew through the air. Pain shot through her as they landed with a jolting crash.

The coppery tang of blood filled her nostrils. Something sharp was in her eye. An elbow? Her head throbbed. She struggled to sit up, but the hot weight of bodies pressed her down. Next to her, she felt someone push at her. "Get off! Get off!" a girl shrieked.

Pressing her hand to her aching head, Ruth untangled her limbs from the shrieking girl. She watched as others untwisted and sat up. Joseph staggered up against the soot-stained wall and limped to the elevator doors. He pulled the chain link door open while some of the other passengers helped. Ruth teetered to her feet. Blood trickled down the doors and a hand tumbled over the top of the car. She gasped as she realized what the thumps overhead had been. The crowd surged forward again, carrying Ruth along to the front doors of the building.

The street swarmed around her as the crowd emptied onto the sidewalk. Screams pierced the air. Fire engine bells clanged. Firemen barked directions. She looked to the building and saw the ladders didn't reach the fire—they only reached the sixth floor.

Onlookers surrounded the building with an indistinct buzz of pointing and speaking in hushed tones. The smell of charred flesh was suffocating. She stepped back and felt something cold and wet slosh over her foot. She forced herself to look down at the sidewalk. Bodies lay in awkward angles from where they had fallen from the sky. The firemen ran around with only two nets, trying to catch people. But there were just too many people to catch. As she watched, another body fell.

She couldn't bring herself to look at the faces lying on the sidewalk, yet she had to.

She had to find them.

Some faces were unrecognizable from their crash on the hard pavement. She forced her feet to move and picked her way across the mass carnage, through the coins and personal effects strewn across the street from the pockets of the falling victims. Scavengers were already running through, gathering all they could into their pockets.

Tears ran down Ruth's face as she recognized the gold crucifix necklace around a bloodied body's neck. Filomena. Something silver caught the sun. She knelt and picked it up. Yankel's metal flask. She looked to her right and saw an unrecognizable body, broken and burnt. She ran her fingers along the edge of Yankel's flask. How many times had she seen Yankel and Abraham pass it back and forth while they stood in the cold on the picket line?

She didn't see Ester or Abraham on the sidewalk. Relief washed through her. But where were they?

She forced herself to look up at the towering inferno.

A girl leaned out an open window on the ninth

floor—the girl from the kindergarten corner Ruth had caught with Grosevich. She screamed as she launched herself, skirt blazing, into the air. Ruth watched as she hit the ground with a sickening thud. Ruth cringed.

Then a flutter of movement and a familiar flash of blue caught her eye from above. There he stood in the ninth-floor window. The same rumpled blue shirt and chestnut hair she'd been admiring a half hour earlier.

"No!" Ruth's arms reached up. "Abraham, don't!"

She watched with horror as Ester joined Abraham in the window. His hand reached up and tenderly stroked Ester's cheek. Ruth shook her head in confusion as she saw him lean in to Ester. Was he kissing her? They broke apart, laced their fingers together and then leapt into the air.

"No!"

Ruth sobbed and collapsed to the sidewalk, unable to look away from her sister and fiancé, together in a heap on the sidewalk, mere inches away from the net.

Their hands were still clasped together.

R u t h

Sunday March 26ᵗʰ, 1911

1 Day After the Fire

Ruth shivered and pulled her coat tighter as a breeze blew from the river. Waiting with her parents, she surveyed the hundreds of others outside the covered pier on Twenty-Sixth Street. A man smoked a cigarette with a pile of stubs already at his feet. Another nervously paced the length of the line, counting his steps as he passed. An older woman stood wrapped in a black shawl, clutching a set of

Rosary beads while she whispered a prayer. Ruth felt the tension radiating off all of them. She wrapped her arms around herself. Her stomach flipped at the thought of what lay ahead.

The pier had been designated the claiming place for bodies from the fire. Ruth knew she'd find Ester and Abraham inside. But what about Mirele, Zusa or Chayele? Had anyone she loved gotten out? Inside were answers, but those answers would dash any hope.

Police officers pushed their way through to the entrance, interrupting the eerie quiet. "We need a line, people. We know this is hard and awful, but it will all be over faster with a line!"

Ruth felt a surge of anger at their presence. How dare they! Just a year ago these police officers beat the picketers—including many of the victims inside. Now they were here trying to offer consolation? Oh, how the world turned!

Momme sniffed next to her, and Ruth took her hand while Tatty tutted softly. Her mother seemed to have shrunk overnight, becoming this fragile bird who might break at the slightest touch. Ruth couldn't remember how she'd gotten home yesterday. Somehow her feet must have brought her there. When she walked in the door, Momme had thrown her arms around Ruth and squeezed till she could barely breathe, before surfacing to look for Ester. Ruth couldn't speak—all she could do was shake her head no and watch her mother shatter. The night was torture as she tossed and turned on the now cavernous couch, listening to her mother grieve another child.

This morning was even worse. Abraham's mother, Sarah, was inconsolable. She couldn't even bring herself to get off the floor where she'd slept. She'd railed against the cruelty of being reunited only to lose him the next day. Samuel had waved them off, saying he needed to send for a doctor to subdue her.

The line finally began moving and they shuffled into the pier. Inside, they were greeted by another police officer who directed them to walk the rows of bodies until they could make an identification.

"There's one hundred and forty-six here. Take your time. Some will be harder to identify, depending on the body's condition."

Ruth gagged and choked back bile as she looked down at the victims. The smell of burned flesh and death engulfed her. All around her people covered their faces with handkerchiefs and rags.

Momme suddenly dropped Ruth's hand and dashed away to the corner, gagging. Ruth looked over to Tatty, but he shrugged helplessly. Taking a deep breath, Ruth squelched down her own horror and ran after Momme.

She leaned over Momme's hunched form and patted her on the back. "You all right?"

She turned away as Momme gagged again in response. Waves of nausea threatened Ruth, but she pinched her nose and forced herself to ignore them. Finally, Momme straightened and wiped her mouth. She teetered for a moment before nodding to Ruth.

"I'm ready."

They rejoined Tatty in the line. Momme clutched Ruth's hand in a vise-like grip, but Ruth didn't try to break it. She glanced down at the bodies surrounding them. Some she recognized immediately. Girls from the table across from her. Jacob who worked on the cutter's table with Abraham. And Mrs. Rossetti, the secretary from the ninth-floor office, who always had homemade treats on her desk.

Some of the faces were recognizable, unburned. Were those the ones who had not paused to jump? The girl from the kindergarten hesitated, if only briefly. Ruth remembered her startled face as she burst into flames before launching into the air. Ruth shook her head, trying to dislodge the image.

The line meandered through the rows. People

stopped to identify their loved ones, and nurses would tag the victim's foot and write down the name. The line stopped as people faltered and dithered over the most distorted faces, trying to make an identification based on clothing or jewelry alone.

Ruth found Chayele standing over one of those bodies. Yankel. He was charred beyond recognition. But sticking out the left pocket of his partially burned pants was his engraved flask. It was the only thing that identified him. Ruth whispered a quick prayer of thanks that she'd remembered to return the flask to the spot she'd found it in the midst of the chaos the day before. She caught Tatty's eye. He nodded and took Momme's hand so Ruth could join her friend. She put her hand on Chayele's shoulder and patted it gently.

Chayele's voice seemed to come from far away. "He was all I had left. And now he's gone too."

Ruth could think of nothing to say. They watched silently as the nurse wrapped the tag around Yankel's foot and added his name.

Ruth hugged Chayele tightly before guiding her back into the line, where they joined Momme and Tatty in the procession moving forward. As they made their way down the fifth row, Tatty stopped and pointed. Ruth closed her eyes and her teeth chattered.

This was it. She hadn't told the family about Ester and Abraham's last moment. Their deaths were shock enough. What if they were still holding hands?

But when she forced herself to open her eyes and look where Tatty pointed, she saw their hands were no longer joined. They now just lay side by side in the row. Tatty identified them and the tags were added.

"It looks like they didn't suffer too much," Chayele said. "I mean, at least they didn't *burn,* you know?"

Ruth shot Chayele an incredulous look and jerked a hand to her mouth to smother a sudden, inappropriate laugh at Chayele's ridiculous statement. At the whole situation. How could they compare suffering and death? How could they be here, identifying Ester and Abraham? This had to be a bad dream, right?

Out of the corner of her eye she saw Tatty wipe away a tear. Would her parents be able to recover from this? They'd now lost *two* children. Ruth had yet to cry. She wanted to; she knew she *should.* But so far she'd felt lost in a fog.

Looking down at their bodies, she felt a swirling confusion. Anger tainted her loss. Had they betrayed her? Had she imagined it? How unfair was it that she could never hear their side of the story?

The four of them forced themselves to leave Ester and Abraham's bodies. Ruth's attention was drawn to a large family a few spaces ahead, surrounding one of the bodies. An elderly woman cried and was being held up by a younger man. Two other women buried their faces in each other's shoulders.

"That's Filomena's family," Chayele said.

"Should we speak to them?"

Chayele shook her head, her chin trembling.

"Ruth?" Tatty tugged on her arm. "If we're done here, I'm going to get your mother outside."

"Ya. There's nothing left here."

"Wait," Chayele pulled her back. "Zusa and Mirele. They have no family to claim them."

Ruth swallowed. Was there no end to the terrible duties of this day? "Are we sure they didn't make it out?"

"I haven't heard from them." Chayele looked over her shoulder at the line of people in the rows.

"We'll wait outside," Tatty said.

Chayele clutched Ruth's arm and pulled her through that row and into the next. The line slowed down. As they waited, an old man with a gray beard and blue, watery eyes joined the couple in front of them. "These last two rows were found in the elevator shafts," Ruth overheard him say. She trembled. The sound of the thumps on the roof of the car still echoed in her head.

Chayele shook her arm. "Look, it's Mirele."

Mirele's neck was positioned in an unnatural angle and her face and arms were shaded with dark bruises. But she was recognizable. Ruth nodded and the nurse tagged Mirele's foot.

They continued to shuffle along with the line to the last row of bodies. But there was no sign of Zusa. As they got to the exit, a police officer noticed Chayele's panicked face.

"Check the hospitals. Victims were sent all over the city." He said gently. "She could be one of the lucky ones."

Chayele nodded, trying to smile.

"If you still can't find her, come back tomorrow. It'll be easier with the claimed bodies gone."

"Thank you, we'll do that," Ruth said.

She squeezed Chayele's hand and steered her into the cool afternoon air. A breeze blew, sweeping Ruth's hair across her face. The street buzzed with energy as people chatted and shopped at the fish market. All traces of the horror inside were shockingly absent.

Tatty and Momme waiting across the street. Momme sat on the curb with her head between her legs. Ruth hurried over to her mother's side.

"We need to get her home," Tatty said, helping her to her feet. "Did you find your friends?"

"One of them. We need to contact hospitals to look for the other," Ruth said.

Tatty turned to Chayele. "I understand you're alone now."

Chayele stared at the ground and nodded.

He put a hand on her shoulder. "You can come stay with us. No one should feel completely alone."

Chayele met his eyes. "Thank you, sir."

He nodded stiffly and turned back to Momme. "Come then. It's been a long day."

Chayele tucked her hand in Ruth's arm and they hurried to keep up with Momme and Tatty.

✳ ✳ ✳

Hours later, during the dark night, Ruth sat in the chair by the window, staring out to the sleepy city. The light from the streetlamps resembled a line of candles, breaking up the otherwise pitch black of the night. A lone carriage clomped its way down the street.

On the couch behind her, Chayele woke and

murmured sleepily, "Can't sleep? What time is it?"

"I don't know. I've been up for a while."

Chayele yawned. "Are you having flashbacks?"

"I keep picturing them together," Ruth whispered.

Chayele crossed the room and put her hand on Ruth's shoulder. "I'm so sorry. I can't imagine how hard that must have been. Helplessly having to watch them."

Ruth turned in the chair to face Chayele. "No, you don't understand. I saw them together. They were *together*."

Chayele tilted her head. "Ruth—"

"I saw them kissing. They kissed and then jumped, holding hands."

She turned away to face the window as Chayele slid down to her knees on the floor next to the chair. Clutching Ruth's hand, Chayele squeezed it tightly between her own.

"You must be mistaken."

Ruth shook her head.

They sat in silence for a moment. Each stared ahead, lost in thought. Finally, Chayele cleared her throat.

"They were caught up in the moment. The fear, the adrenaline. They were seeking comfort."

Ruth shook her head as Chayele spoke. "I don't

think so. It was more. They were so intimate." She swallowed hard. "I think I'm... responsible."

Chayele pulled her shawl around her shoulders. "How? How could you possibly be responsible for your fiancé and your sister betraying you?"

Ruth sighed. "For not listening. For ignoring their needs while I got so involved with the union and the suffragettes. They kept telling me I was pushing them away. I just didn't see I was pushing them to each other." She plucked at the hem of her nightgown in her lap. "Abraham wanted to feel needed. He even mentioned a few times how nice it was that Ester did need him. Maybe that was his way of telling me."

Chayele readjusted herself on the floor so her back could lean against the wall. "I doubt it was that simple, even if it was going on as long as you suspect. Abraham was an honorable man, Ruth. And whether he was confused or not, he did care for you. And Ester was your sister..." She shook her head. "I don't believe it. Even if they had feelings for each other, I refuse to believe they acted on them before that moment."

Ruth didn't answer. They sat in silence again. Ruth stared out the window as the sun poked its head out in the distance from behind the corners of buildings. Chayele fiddled with the edge of her shawl, twirling it round and round her finger. Finally, Ruth's broke the silence with a trembling voice.

"Do you know what the worst part is?"

"What?"

"I want to be angry. I really do. And a part of me definitely is. But another part wonders if maybe they *should* have been together. She obviously loved him in a way I never did."

"How can you possibly know that?" Chayele asked.

"She left the elevator, Chayele. She ran back into the burning building to be with him! All I thought of was getting myself out."

"Oh, Ruth," Chayele grabbed Ruth's hand. "That doesn't mean you loved him less. It just means you wanted to survive. You preserved yourself. That's natural."

"For me, apparently. That's what they both complained about me doing all the time. But Ester— Ester sprang right out of that elevator and ran against the crowd, back into the flames. To get to him."

"I can't think of many people who would have done that, so you can't compare yourself to her. No one can predict how someone will react in a situation like that." Chayele turned her head away from Ruth to stare at the wall. "I didn't think of anyone else that day. I just ran. I didn't look back at all. Does that call into question my love for my brother or my friends? Maybe. All I can say is, as much as I grieve for Yankel, Filomena and Mirele, I'm still glad I made it out alive."

Ruth turned back to the window. Chayele climbed into the chair next to her and wrapped her arms around Ruth. Ruth leaned her head on Chayele's shoulder. They were both silent as they watched the sunrise fill the sky in the distance.

R u t h

Ruth woke to the sound of rain pounding against the window. She sighed. It had been raining for days. Appropriately fitting her mood, but also a true annoyance. Today was the union funeral procession for all the victims from the fire. It would be even more depressing to march in this weather.

She lifted herself over Chayele's sleeping form. She really should start sleeping on the empty cot in the kitchen. It was silly to continue sharing the couch with Chayele when there was a perfectly good bed in the next room. But Ruth could not bring herself to take over Abraham's space like that.

That seemed to be how everyone felt. Samuel had moved Sarah and the children to an apartment upstairs. He said they needed the space to grieve in private. They all did.

Ruth pulled her shawl around her shoulders and entered the empty kitchen. She'd heard Momme up with the teething baby most of the night, so she tried to light the fire as quietly as possible, savoring the warmth as the flames grew. It was funny, the complicated relationship people had with fire. She'd never forget the power and danger of those licking flames in the factory, but she was glad to have the pleasure of a fire's warmth on a chilly morning.

She filled the tea kettle and placed it on the stove. As she waited for the water to boil, she sat at the table and gazed at the dishes Ester had helped Momme artfully arrange on the shelves, and the wooden animals Abraham had carved and lined along a shelf above his bed. Ester and Abraham's presence was felt everywhere. A wooden box sitting on the fireplace mantel caught Ruth's eye. That was new. She crossed the room to examine it.

Ester's name was written on the box. Cracking it open, Ruth found an assortment of items from her sister's childhood. A wooden doll Jeremiah had carved for her. Pressed flowers from their garden in St. Petersburg. A wooden bird. Had Jeremiah carved that also? Ruth looked to the wooden animals above Abraham's bed and noted the similarities. A spark of anger flooded her. She stuffed the bird back into the box and saw the journal Momme had given Ester for her birthday tucked in the corner. Opening it, she saw that Ester had filled most of the pages.

Ruth was interrupted by the sound of the water boiling. After pouring herself a fragrant, steaming cup of tea, she carried both cup and journal to the table and settled in to read. A wave of shame flooded her as she read the first entry.

Ruth abandoned me AGAIN today. On my birthday! What must I do to warrant her attention? I remember the days back in Russia when she would smother me with concern and affection. I'd go back to those hard times for just a moment of Ruth's uninterrupted attention again.

Ruth felt like she'd been punched in the stomach. Had she really been so callous? Had Ester been punishing her with Abraham?

She turned the page and read on.

Today I was accepted into the fall class of the Jewish Teacher's College! I'm going to be a teacher!

A teacher? Ester? Ruth's brow knit. And what was this Jewish Community Reform group Ester had been attending? Had Ester been her own sort of activist? It seemed she had been leading a whole life that Ruth knew nothing about.

She stiffened as a hand touched her shoulder.

"Sorry, I didn't mean to startle you." Momme said with a yawn.

Ruth smiled. "I was so engrossed I didn't hear you. Do you want some tea?"

"Ya, I'd love that. Thanks."

Ruth jumped to her feet. When she returned to the table with the tea, she saw that Momme had pulled the journal to where she sat and was examining it.

"I remember when I got this for Ester for her birthday," Momme said. "She had so many exciting adventures coming up. I wanted her to have someplace to document them all."

Ruth passed the cup. "You knew about the Teacher's College?"

Momme blew on the hot tea. "Of course." She frowned at Ruth. "Didn't you?"

"I think there was a lot I may have missed." Ruth played with the handle of her tea cup.

Momme reached across the table and put her hand on top of Ruth's. "Grief is hard enough without adding guilt into the mix. You were a good sister. She knew you loved her."

Ruth felt her eyes well up and reached up with the back of her hand to wipe them away.

Momme stood and wrapped her arms around Ruth. Ruth patted Momme's arm, wishing it was that simple. Wishing she could just let it go, knowing she'd been good enough to them both. But Momme hadn't seen what Ruth had. And Ruth wasn't about to add this burden to Momme's own load. No, she had to be strong and bear it alone.

She sniffled and cleared her throat. "So, what did you think about Ester's plans?"

Momme shrugged and sat back down at the table. "At first I thought she'd taken leave of her senses. Girls attending *yeshiva* with boys?" She shook her head, and Ruth raised her eyebrows.

"But she kept at it, pushing me, asking questions, forcing me to think about Judaism and my identity. She really wanted to ensure our culture would not be lost here in America."

Ruth frowned. "Didn't she want to be an American?"

Momme shook her head. "Oh no, she did! She was amazed by the freedoms you were embracing. The voice women have here." Momme gazed unseeing at her cup. "But she was afraid people were embracing those opportunities at the expense of their past. I think it was those English classes that started it. The emphasis everyone placed on English. And then, well…Hedy. She feared young Jewish children in America might never hear or speak Yiddish at all."

Ruth nodded, thinking of her own desperation to fit in. "So, what was she proposing? Jewish children avoid all things American and preserve their culture?"

Momme tilted her head. "Balance. She wanted a new American form of Judaism with the best of both."

The baby started crying and Momme sighed. "That was short-lived." She leaned on the table to stand and returned to the bedroom.

Wrinkling her brow, Ruth continued to page through the journal. Ester had scrawled lines from the *Torah* and what looked like quotes from Jewish Reform leaders in the city. There were also flow charts and outlines of plans she'd been looking to implement. To-do lists with tasks like "go door to door to canvas interest" and "scout future buildings sites". Why didn't Ester share any of her excitement with Ruth? How involved had Ester been in this?

Despite the early hour, Ruth couldn't help herself. She opened the front door and marched down the hall to Hedy's apartment.

Hedy answered the door, bleary-eyed and rumpled from sleep. She rubbed her face and stepped outside to join Ruth in the hallway, closing her apartment door quietly. "I had a feeling you'd come eventually. I take it you found her journal?"

"How did you know about her journal?" Ruth asked sharply.

Hedy flushed. "Your sister and I shared a lot."

"So much she felt she didn't need to confide in her own family?"

Hedy pulled her shawl more tightly around her shoulders. "Ruth, your sister was discovering herself. Who she was, what she wanted. I was just helping her find her voice."

Ruth's voice softened. "How involved in this…this movement was she?"

Hedy sighed. "Her loss will be felt. Your sister was everything and anything. And she was a sponge, always willing to learn more."

"Was she working to be an activist of sorts?"

"No. She was too young. But she had ideas. She took part in meetings, and everyone learned to listen to what she had to say. She understood better than most people that to truly evoke change, you had to see the whole picture, listen to both sides."

"Everyone has a story," Ruth whispered.

"Yes!" Hedy said. "She was always saying that."

"She started saying that as a little girl. When we complained about the grouchy old man at the market, she'd say maybe he has gout, or maybe his wife is ill."

Hedy nodded. "Exactly. It's a talent, to look at the world that way. She inspired everyone working for Jewish reform. She might have still been completing her formal *yeshiva* teacher training, but she was already a teacher."

"Thanks Hedy," Ruth said.

Hedy put a hand on Ruth's arm. "Come visit sometime. Don't be a stranger."

Ruth watched as Hedy turned back to her door. "Wait, Hedy."

Hedy stopped and looked at her.

Ruth's thoughts scrambled. Did she want to know? She sighed. "Did she ever say anything about me?"

Hedy smiled. "Just that she thought the world of

you. You were the sun and moon to her stars, *bubbele*."

Ruth smiled as Hedy stepped back into her apartment and closed the door.

As she walked back to her apartment, she reflected on what she'd learned. She might disagree with Ester's mission—to focus a life around Judaism in America seemed unnecessary and misguided. But she was impressed by how Ester had found a way to use her gifts and work for change in her own way. Her soft-spoken, homebody sister!

She opened the door to the apartment to find everyone up and cluttering the small kitchen. Momme stood at the stove, bouncing the baby on her hip while she attempted to measure oats for oatmeal. Chayele was feeding wood into the stove down by Momme's feet. And Tatty sat at the table reading his siddur prayer book. Ruth took a deep breath and entered the room. She took the baby from her mother and smiled.

R u t h

Ruth woke the morning of the trial to see her breath in front of her face as she exhaled. She threw her feet over the side of the cot and wrapped her shawl tightly around her shoulders. She glanced up to the cut-out to see out through the parlor window and saw the ground blanketed with a half-foot of snow. That would definitely complicate things today. She turned her attention to stoking the fire to heat up the iron. She'd finally started sleeping on the cot in the kitchen a few weeks back. It still felt wrong, even after all this time. But then again, everything in the apartment still felt strange. Even now, she half-expected the front door to open and Ester and Abraham to come walking in, laughing over something funny that happened.

Laying out her shirtwaist and skirt on the ironing board, she went over them three times to make sure they were completely wrinkle-free. Both garments were black, as her attorney, Mr. Bostwick, instructed. The color of mourning. But she didn't need the color to remind her of all she'd lost.

It had been nine months, but her mind still wandered to the image of Abraham cupping Ester's face and kissing her. Chayele and Anne told her the best way she could forgive them and herself was to make their deaths mean something. For that reason, she agreed to testify against Mr. Blanck and Mr. Harris in the trial today. She firmly believed they were stuck on the hook this time. There was no way they could walk away from this.

Finished with the iron, she dressed with care, taking time to smooth and arrange every fold of her outfit. Remembering her lessons from Zusa, she pinned her hair in delicate curls that cascaded like a waterfall down her head. Chayele bustled in just as Ruth finished.

"Ready?" she asked.

Ruth nodded. "As I'll ever be."

The door to her parents' room opened and her mother tiptoed out. She was still in her nightgown, clutching a shawl wrapped tightly round her body. Her long hair hung in a braid over her shoulder.

"You're leaving?" Momme asked. "Did you eat?"

Ruth crossed the room, taking Momme into her arms. Ruth was struck by how sturdy her mother still seemed. She'd lost weight, no doubt. Her skin now hung on her tiny frame. Ruth could have sworn she'd even gotten shorter. There was no way she'd always towered over her mother this way. But Momme hadn't shattered as Ruth had feared. She was still getting up each day and putting one foot in front of the other. Living another day, caring for them all as she always did. Ruth wondered why she hadn't seen it before, but perhaps what she'd always equated to her mother's weakness had in reality been her quiet strength, carrying her through.

Chayele gave her a gentle nudge and Ruth let go. Momme watched silently as they bundled themselves in their coats. They then slipped out the front door and began their descent to the street.

Ruth shook her head and tried to ignore the lingering sadness she felt from leaving her mother.

Chayele put a hand on her arm. "You asked them to come. You did all you could."

Ruth nodded. "I know."

She had begged her parents to come to the trial, but they steadfastly refused. "What does it matter who's to blame?" Tatty murmured, sinking into a chair and opening his copy of the *Torah* with trembling fingers. "That won't help Ester and Abraham find peace. All we can do is pray for them."

Momme stayed silent, but she obviously agreed.

At least they hadn't argued with her about her own decision to take part in the trial.

Anne's car waited for them by the curb out front. Her driver held the door open for the girls.

"How are you doing?" Anne asked as Ruth slid into the back seat.

Ruth tried to smile. "My stomach is doing flips."

"That's expected." Anne squeezed her knee. "Just remember Mr. Bostwick's instructions and it'll be fine."

They drove to the courthouse in silence. Ruth stared out the window at the piles of snow lining the street, and the men with shovels working to clear the way. She prayed the weather would not impact the trial. She couldn't imagine waiting any longer.

They walked in to find a mob in the lobby.

"They're here for Blanck and Harris," Chayele said.

Ruth hoped there wouldn't be a riot. She knew the judge had limited attendance inside the courtroom to people pertinent to the trial, but there was no way to keep people away from the lobby.

"Let us through!" said Anne. "These are official witnesses!" Ruth's heart pounded as they started to press their way through the throng of excited bodies.

Then the elevator doors opened to reveal Mr. Blanck, Mr. Harris, and their lawyer, Max Steur. Ruth felt the current of the mob shift toward the men. She had to resist its force to stay in place.

"Murderers! Murderers!" People booed and flapped papers in Blanck and Harris's faces.

"What are those papers?" Ruth asked.

"Photographs," Anne said. "Of the victims."

For the first time ever, Ruth saw a crack in Mr. Blanck's ice-cold facade. Beads of sweat dripped down his face despite the chilly day. The crowd was getting to him. He was afraid—that much was apparent. Good, she thought, it's about time he felt afraid. Did he feel guilty as well? She couldn't tell.

Anne grabbed Ruth's elbow. "Let's find a seat before they're all taken. You need to try to relax and stay calm, if you can."

Ruth burrowed deeper in her coat as they gave their names to the guard and entered the relative hush of the courtroom. Despite the sunlight streaming in the windows, the room felt almost as cold as the wintry day outside. She could see the breath of the people huddled on the benches in their winter coats. The careful care she took preparing her outfit might prove to be for nothing if the room never warmed.

Clara stood and waved them over to where she sat, saving them seats. Ruth and Chayele gave Clara a hug as they sat down, while Anne and Clara greeted each other with stiff civility.

Blanck and Harris already sat up front, whispering with their lawyer. According to rumor, the men had hired the fanciest lawyer in New York City; Max Steur had his hand in every big case in the news. The prosecutor, Bostwick, had warned Ruth about him and his method of questioning witnesses— he was charming but ruthless, and known for his photographic memory. Seeing him in person, Ruth felt even more nervous about being under his scrutiny on the stand. Short and stocky, he wore a no-nonsense expression and reminded her of an alert fox taking in every detail of his surroundings.

"Ruth!" Chayele elbowed her. Everyone was rising to their feet. Ruth jumped up just as Judge Thomas Crain swept into his seat with an evasive glance over the room, meeting no one's eyes.

The jury filed in, twelve men in suits, some better-fitting than others. Ruth peered around the tall hat feathers of a woman in front of her to try to read their faces, but they were all equally stone-faced.

Bostwick tugged at his bushy mustache and launched into his opening statement. "Gentlemen of the jury, locking a factory door during working hours is a misdemeanor, and a misdemeanor that leads to death is considered felony manslaughter. I set out to prove today that Isaac Harris and Max Blanck knowingly ordered an exit door to be locked on the day of the fire. And in doing so, they are responsible for the deaths of one hundred and forty-six people..."

* * *

"Miss Feldman, could you please tell us what you were doing when the fire began that day?" Mr. Bostwick stroked his mustache and paced before her.

Ruth twisted her handkerchief in her lap. "I was finishing my work for the day at my sewing station with my sister and friends."

"Um, Your Honor, I have to object." Mr. Steur stood. "Not all of the jury members speak Yiddish and will be able to follow Miss Feldman's statement."

Ruth blushed. Mr. Bostwick had warned her of this, but in her nervousness she had lapsed into her comfortable native tongue.

"I have translators available, Your Honor." Mr. Bostwick winked at Ruth.

Steur leapt to his feet again. "I have to object to that as well, Your Honor. How could the jury be sure nothing is lost in translation?"

Judge Crain spoke. "I have to agree. Only English may be spoken in testimony, if witnesses are capable."

Heat rose to Ruth's face. She gave a small nod before repeating her earlier statement in English.

"Was there any warning before you saw the fire erupting from the air shaft?" Bostwick asked.

"No sir. No warning. Just flames coming at us and taking over the floor. We ran... but tables and machines blocked us. So, we got into line in the aisles. But when we got to the Washington Place stairs, the door was locked."

"Locked, you say? Had you ever used this door before that day?" Bostwick asked.

"No sir. We were always told to leave through the Greene Street door so our bags could be checked."

"Then why did you try to leave by the Washington Place door that day?"

"It was closer, sir. And there was already a big crowd of girls by the Greene Street doors."

"What happened when you discovered the door was locked?"

"Everyone—the crowd, sir—was calling to Mr. Grosevich, the foreman. Screaming for him to bring the key. But he never came. He'd already escaped."

"Objection," Steur said. "Speculation."

The judge nodded.

Bostwick offered Ruth a reassuring smile. "So, Mr. Grosevich never came, for unknown reasons. Then what happened?"

She focused on one juror with a curl flopping over his forehead, making him appear younger, more open. "The room was full of smoke. It burned my chest. I pushed onto the elevator—the last one—with my sister, Ester. But she—we were separated at the last minute and she didn't make it on the car." Ruth's voice cracked and she took a deep breath before continuing. "I called for her, but the operator, Joseph

Zito, said no, we couldn't go back. The elevator went down. There were thumps on the ceiling, and the plaster started cracking and falling down on us in the car. Then we heard screams and ripping noises and the elevator started to fall. We crashed down the shaft to the bottom. All of us in the car got out, but the elevator couldn't go up for any more trips."

"Now take a moment Miss Feldman, I understand this is difficult. But what did you see when you got outside to the street?"

"I saw..." Tears erupted and she struggled to take in a calming breath. "I saw my sister and fiancé trapped in the window of the ninth floor. When the fire came close to them, they both jumped. They—they fell to the ground in front of me."

She looked down at her lap, unable to meet Mr. Bostwick's eyes. Would they know she was leaving out an important detail? But it was personal, not relevant to the case.

"Miss Feldman, in addition to you sister and fiancé, how many people did you see jump from the windows?"

"I don't know exactly," Ruth stuttered.

"As many as ten, possibly?" Bostwick gently pushed.

"Yes," she sighed. "More than ten."

"More than twenty?"

"Yes."

"Thirty perhaps?" he continued.

"Your Honor, I object to this!" Steur jumped to his feet. "May I approach the bench, please?"

Ruth dabbed at her eyes with the handkerchief as the two lawyers approached the judge.

She heard whispered snippets of their argument. Steur mentioned something about a bias against his client, and Bostwick said something about it being emotionally vital to the case. Finally, Judge Crain sent them both back to their seats.

"From this point forward there will be no mention of events occurring after the outbreak of the fire. Only events leading up to and during the actual outbreak may be discussed. There will be no mention of escapes or actual witnessing of deaths."

From the corner of her eye, Ruth saw Chayele drop her head into her hands and Clara put an arm around her shoulders. How could the judge do this? How would the ruling impact the case?

"As you wish, Your Honor." Bostwick bowed. He chewed his lip as he considered his next move. Finally, he looked up and met Ruth's eyes again.

"Thank you, Miss Feldman. That will be all."

She looked at Steur. She expected him to jump up and interrogate her, but instead he met her gaze with a sly smile and said she had already answered his questions. Her legs shook, but she somehow managed to return to her seat next to Anne and Chayele without stumbling. She'd expected the butterflies in her stomach to mellow now that her testimony was done, but instead she felt like they'd morphed into bats or birds, trapped and flapping around in there.

"Don't worry, dear. Mr. Bostwick will find a way to redirect his efforts," Anne said, patting her hand. Ruth tried to convince herself to remain confident.

A few moments later, Mr. Blanck was called to the stand. Ruth sent him an icy glare as he passed her, but he never even looked her way. She twisted her hands in her lap as he took his oath and settled into his seat. This was it. Time for Bostwick to expose him for what he really was.

"Mr. Blanck, could you please tell the court what you were doing when the fire began?" Steur asked.

"I was standing in the shipping department on the tenth floor. Somebody called out that my taxi had arrived. You see, it was Saturday, and I was supposed to be taking my daughters shopping that afternoon. I'd left them in my office with their governess, so I started heading in that direction to get the girls when I saw someone running through the hallway yelling there was a fire on the eighth floor. I ran to the Greene Street door to check on the situation, but I then—"

He paused, and his forehead furrowed. "I remembered my girls. I was afraid they'd be frightened, so I turned back for them. Together, we headed for the elevator... But when I got there all the pressers were stampeding to the elevator, yelling, 'Save us! Save us!' So I loaded all the pressers into the elevator and told the operator to take them all down and come straight back."

Steur turned to the jury. "Let me clarify. You loaded your employees—all of them—onto the elevators while remaining behind yourself with your daughters?"

Mr. Blanck paused to take a big breath and glanced around the courtroom. "Yes, sir. I did."

"What happened after that?" Steur pressed.

"I stood there waiting for the elevator to return, but it felt like it was taking forever. And at that point, with my girls holding both my hands, all I could think was I didn't have any minutes to spare. So, I ran to the other side and opened the Washington Place door."

"And that door opened? Meaning it was unlocked?" Steur asked.

"Oh yes, it opened right away."

"Were you holding a key?" Steur turned to the jury.

Max looked to the jury as well. "No, I did not have a key with me. It was unlocked."

"Then what happened?"

"I meant to run downstairs, but when I looked down the stairs all I could see was smoke. I knew the children wouldn't be able to stand it. From somewhere behind me I heard Isaac yelling that we had to run up to the roof. I looked back at the smoky stairwell again and knew that was our only option. I grabbed my two girls by the hand and up to the roof we ran. We were later rescued by some NYU students in the next building who used a ladder as a bridge between the buildings to cross to safety."

"What a story of heroes!" Mr. Steur exclaimed. "But to clarify once more. The staircase you examined, it was filled with smoke and impassable?"

Mr. Blanck nodded. "Yes, sir. There was no way to go down that staircase. You could feel the heat as soon as you opened the door."

"Thank you, I have no further questions," Mr. Steur said, turning away from Mr. Blanck to the jury.

"What a load of hooey," Chayele muttered.

Clara rolled her eyes. "And the perfect father act?"

Bostwick did his best to poke holes in Blanck's story, but the jury members' faces remained impassive.

Anne leaned over and gestured to the jury as Blanck left the stand. "Tough bunch."

Ruth bit her lip. They still had Mr. Harris to question. It wasn't over yet. She leaned forward as Steur approached Harris to begin.

"Mr. Harris, how long have you and Mr. Blanck been business partners?" Steur asked.

"Twelve years, sir. His wife is my cousin."

"A family business then, how nice. And what was your responsibility in the business?"

"I was mainly the designer. I came up with the product designs and looked after everything on the floors." Harris explained.

Steur clasped his hands behind his back. "So, you were on the floor for most of the day?"

"Yes, sir. I spent most days traveling from floor to floor. I divided my time among the three floors."

"How did you get between floors? The elevator?"

"Oh no, sir," Harris shook his head. "It was

much faster to take the stairs."

"And which staircase did you take? The Greene Street stairs or the Washington Place?" Steur asked.

"Both, sir. Whichever one was closer, depending on which side of the building I was on at the time."

"Did you carry a key with you?"

"No, my key was left in my office. Both staircase doors were always unlocked."

"If you didn't carry a key, who was in charge of locking up each day?" Steur asked.

"The foreman, Mr. Grosevich, sir. He opened each day and locked up each night along with two other watchmen."

"Thank you, Mr. Harris. That is all." Steur smiled and sat down.

Bostwick rose to his feet.

"In your twelve years as partners, did you suffer from any other fires, Mr. Harris?"

"Yes," Harris said slowly. "But that's normal in any large factory, Mr. Bostwick."

"Possibly, but are you aware there's some coincidental timing in all your fires?" Bostwick turned back to the papers on his table.

Harris frowned. "I'm not sure what you mean."

"Well, let's start with this: how many other fires

317

do you recollect there being, Mr. Harris?"

Harris shifted his weight in his seat and looked down at his lap. "Two, I believe."

"Two that were reported to insurance you mean, Mr. Harris." Bostwick opened the file he was holding. "As far as I can tell from employee testimony, there have actually been at least four fires."

"Two of them were nothing more than waste basket fires. They were put out almost immediately."

Bostwick stroked his mustache and flicked his gaze to the ceiling. "Ah, yes…it's a shame you had such—ah, *diligent* employees on those two occasions."

Harris sputtered, "We rewarded those employees handsomely. We've trained all our employees to be safety conscious and installed a state-of-the art fire prevention system."

"A system not properly maintained, or anything more than smoke and mirrors. Which is interesting with your history. All four of these fires just happened to coincide with the end of your busy seasons, when you had excess inventory. All of which was conveniently insured." Bostwick snapped the file closed and leaned closer to Harris. "What was the game here? You couldn't sell the leftover products so you'd make the money back by setting a fire and collecting a nice insurance check?"

Ruth gasped. Was Bostwick suggesting ownership had started the fire on purpose?

Steur jumped to his feet. "Objection, Your Honor!"

Bostwick pushed away from where he was leaning and held up his hands in surrender.

"Withdrawn."

But as he walked back to his table to replace the file, there was a gleam in his eye.

"That can't be true, can it? They wouldn't really have set the fire on purpose with all of us in the building?" Ruth whispered to Chayele.

Chayele shook her head. "No, they were in the building too. Blanck even had his little girls there."

Anne leaned in. "But he's planting a seed of doubt. That's all we need for the jury."

Ruth twirled a curly lock of hair.

The trial continued for days, with testimony from hundreds of witnesses. All gave conflicting reports about the locked door. Steur, with his incredible memory, was quick to leap on witnesses for either changing their facts or for even repeating them too perfectly.

"Are you sure you never gave this testimony before?" he berated one girl.

"No, sir. This is the first time."

"Tell it to me again, just as you told it before."

Nervously, the girl fumbled through her testimony again. It became obvious as he walked her through her account four times on the stand that she was repeating key phrases. What was probably a rehearsed speech at home was now looking like a coached statement.

He turned around and slammed the railing in front of the jury box. "Do you see, gentlemen? The similarities in her story? How do we know this alleged locked door has not just been made up and rehearsed in meetings with union leaders?"

He twirled back around to the shaking girl on the stand. "Isn't it true you received a letter in October to appear at a meeting with the lawyer for the Ladies' Waist and Dressmakers' Union?"

"No, sir," the girl's voice trembled.

"You didn't meet with a lawyer to prepare?"

The girl's eyes glistened. "No, sir, I swear."

He turned and let it go, but Ruth could tell the jury was considering the idea.

At last, the lawyers recited their closing statements. Steur reiterated the owners had no knowledge of a locked door and even so, it was not the door that prevented the workers from leaving the building, but a smoky, impassable inferno in the stairwell itself.

Bostwick reiterated that the owners were most definitely aware of the locked door, and multiple witnesses had testified that the same locked door forced them to find another way to escape. He reminded the jury that one hundred and forty-six people died that day, and the owners needed to be held accountable for their part in the conditions that caused those deaths.

After he sat down, the courtroom remained silent for a few moments. Judge Crain cleared his throat.

"This has been a difficult case, dealing with an extremely emotional ordeal. Gentlemen of the jury, you have a heavy responsibility, one which not many would envy. But before you enter deliberation, I need to remind you the letter of the law dictates you only consider the actual charges at hand. You cannot consider emotions or past allegations."

He folded his hands in front of him and took a deep breath. "In this particular case, because they are charged with a felony, I remind you that before you find these defendants guilty of manslaughter in the first degree, you must find that the door was in fact locked. If it was locked, it must have been locked with the defendants' knowledge. You must also decide without a reasonable doubt that such locking caused the deaths of the victims in the fire. If you cannot make a direct correlation between these two events, you cannot find the defendants guilty. We await your verdict."

The jury filed out to the deliberation room as the courtroom erupted into discussions.

"They have to find them guilty, right?" Ruth asked.

Clara shook her head. "I'm not sure. The jury loves Steur."

Chayele shook her head. "No, no. They have to convict. There's no way they can get away with this."

Anne squeezed Ruth's hand. "Deep breaths, Ruth. We're just going to have to wait and see."

Three hours later, the jury filed in to a silent courtroom.

Judge Crain rubbed his forehead. "Have you come to a verdict?"

Ruth took a deep breath. She grabbed Anne and Chayele's hands.

The foreman stood. "Yes, Your Honor. In response to the charges, we the jury find the defendants not guilty."

Ruth felt a terrible coldness spread through her as the shouting from the gallery hit her with a crash.

Her vision blurred, but she saw Judge Crain jump to his feet and gesture urgently for the guards to escort the jury out the back door.

Other guards hustled Blanck and Harris away, to move them to a safe location Ruth supposed, as the stomping and screaming grew.

Ruth sat stunned in the midst of the chaos. How was this possible? After all the sacrifices and time she'd committed, Blanck and Harris were walking free. It was all for nothing.

"Ruth?" Chayele prodded her shoulder. "Have you heard a word Clara said? We need to head to union headquarters for an emergency meeting. If we start now, we can get a protest organized by Monday."

"No more protests! We need to get a petition circulating," Anne shouted.

Ruth looked at the darkening window and suddenly everything felt crystal clear. She gathered her belongings and got to her feet. Turning to face Chayele, Clara and Anne, she frowned. "I'm sorry, there's someplace else I need to be."

"What?" Chayele tilted her head in confusion.

Ruth ran from the courtroom.

R u t h

Ruth pushed her way through the crowds in the streets, her only priority to put distance between herself and the courthouse. The cold air invaded her nostrils and burned as it filled her lungs. Words echoed through her mind as she quickened her pace.

You live with the dead. Those were Samuel's words, delivered years ago, during the strike. Ruth had dismissed his accusation almost without consideration.

You're pushing us all away. That was Abraham. Ruth had always been too busy to listen. She always thought they'd have their entire lives to grow closer.

Ruth abandoned me AGAIN today. On my birthday! What must I do to warrant Ruth's attention? Ester, a year before she died.

Ruth's gut ached with guilt, remembering the words of the people she professed to love.

All that time, lost. Her relationships, lost. And for what? A cause proven to be fruitless.

She turned the corner to Orchard Street and saw the pushcart vendors packing up for the day. She threw open the door to her building and took the stairs two at a time. Bursting into the apartment, she found Tatty and Momme seated at the kitchen table with the Sabbath candles between them. Momme had the baby on her lap. They looked up, startled, as she crossed the room and sat across from them. Without a word, Tatty reached across the table and took her hand in his. She squeezed his fingers and bowed her head as Momme lit the candles and Tatty recited the *Shabbat* prayers

Ruth woke the next morning to her mother shaking her arm.

"Look, look!" Momme flapped a newspaper.

Ruth rubbed her eyes and yawned. She sat up on the cot and looked around the kitchen. Her parents' bedroom door stood open; Tatty must have already gone upstairs to visit Samuel.

Momme poured a cup of tea for Ruth and brought it to the kitchen table, where she smoothed out the newspaper. She gestured for Ruth to come over.

Ruth sighed and dragged herself to the table. Her eyes felt gritty and dry. She'd tossed and turned all night, thinking of the injustice of the verdict. She slumped into the chair and took a sip of fragrant tea before glancing down at the *Jewish Daily Forward*. On the front page was a collage of photographs, one of which was her own face.

Momme grinned and pointed to her picture. "It's you!" she gushed. "They're calling you a hero."

"A hero?" Ruth stuttered. "But, they tossed out half my testimony."

She focused on the Yiddish headline before skimming through the rest of the article.

Shirtwaist Kings Relinquish Their Crowns!

Momme slid into the chair across from Ruth. "See? You told your story and made a difference!"

Ruth leaned back in the chair and crossed her arms. "This says the trial brought attention to their corruption, but most people already knew about that."

"Then you must not be reading the whole article, Ruth. It says a lot more. People are talking about taking down the entire corrupt Tammany system. Everyone knows that judge was paid off."

Ruth sighed. "So what? They're going to start protesting like we did back in Russia? Demand reform of the corrupt system? Weren't you the ones lecturing me the job would never be done, there would always be another enemy to fight?"

Momme nodded. "That is true. But perhaps this *is* finally different. The government already formed that Factory Investigating Committee back in June."

Ruth gulped down the last of her tea and stood. She walked to the stove and scooped a spoonful of the porridge waiting there into a bowl. Momme watched, waiting for her to speak. When she didn't, Momme got to her feet and put her hand on Ruth's arm.

"This isn't you." She waved a hand over the table. "There's a backlash…isn't that progress? Of a kind."

"Since when do you care about progress?"

Momme tilted her head. "I watched my two daughters try to improve the world. In different ways—very different ways. But things are getting better. Shouldn't we embrace that?"

She dug into her pocket and pulled out two nickels. Sliding them onto the counter, she leaned over and kissed Ruth on the cheek. "I'm proud of you. Why don't you and Chayele go out to the pictures tonight to celebrate? Try and start living again, ya?"

She turned and walked into her bedroom, leaving Ruth alone in the kitchen. Ruth took a spoonful of porridge and stared down at the two nickels on the counter. Was Momme right? Had she become too cynical to see change occurring? After that verdict was announced yesterday, all she could think about was the wasted time and mess she'd made of everything. How she'd managed to ruin all that had been good in her life. But maybe it was time to make a fresh start. The nickelodeon might not be the happiest choice though. She had never gone without Abraham.

She put down her bowl and plopped back onto the cot to think. Some things from under the mattress fell to the floor. Reaching to gather them, she found the dime novel Filomena had given her two years before. Abraham must have stuffed it under there after he confiscated it. She had yet to learn to read in English.

Well, why not start now? Leaning back on the pillow, she settled in to make herself comfortable and opened the book to the first page.

R u t h

The heavy metal door clanked shut behind her. Ruth tensed, and the guard snickered.

"Sure you're up for this?"

Ruth straightened to her full height and brushed at her skirt. She tried to give the guard a stony look. "Lead the way, sir."

He shrugged and stepped ahead to lead her down the gloomy stone hallway. Gas lights flickered every few feet, throwing out brief glowing respites from the otherwise pitch black that surrounded them. The stone façade broke way to cells lining each side. Men stood, clutching the bars, offering jeers and catcalls as she walked by. Ruth kept her eyes straight ahead, refusing to show any weakness by reacting. Finally, the guard stopped and jerked his head in the direction of a cell. He turned with his hand outstretched and she dropped the agreed-upon payment in his hand. She cleared her throat. He grumbled and handed over his lamp as well, then strolled away, leaving her on her own.

Ruth squinted to make out Blanck's hunched form on a cot. She took a hesitant step to the bars.

His voice rang out, as self-assured and booming as ever. "I somehow knew it would be you who'd come." He reached a hand to the wall and pulled himself up. "I've followed your articles in the *Jewish Daily Forward*. You've made a name for yourself."

He stepped closer. "But, you always were a chattering nuisance."

She met his eyes and smiled. "One who appears to finally be on the winning side."

Blanck chuckled. "Momentarily."

Ruth set down the lantern and got out her notebook and pen. *Don't let him rattle you.* She was here to get his story, and she would.

"You're in jail. The fire inspector *caught* you locking the door this time. But someone wise once told me there were two sides to every story. So, what do you have to say for yourself?"

Blanck leaned in closer to the bars. She could smell his stale breath and unwashed body. "Where were you from in Russia? St. Petersburg?" he asked.

She nodded slightly.

"I was from Bialystok," he said. "One of the small villages outside the city. You're too young to remember the burnings. Funny actually, how fires have been such important features of my life."

"Enlighten me," she said. "Did the burnings bring you to America?"

"June 10th, 1890. That was the day my life changed. I woke to a torch flying through my window, landing inches from my bed. Outside a mob swarmed, burning everything in their path. My family and I escaped, each running in different directions, praying we'd make it through the night."

He glanced at Ruth, looking for her reaction. But she refused to give him one. Keeping her face down, she remained impassive, scrawling notes.

"Ever spend a night in a tree?"

Ruth shook her head.

"Those stupid fools never thought to look up. But I spent that whole night afraid to make a sound, afraid to doze off and fall among those wretched Russian peasants below me. They didn't stop until the entire village was one huge roaring fire. And even the fire wasn't enough! They surrounded and beat my neighbors as they fled their flaming houses. The terror just dragged on. I finally just closed my eyes until the morning light flickered and the noise subsided.

"I climbed down and looked around at the wreckage. Shells of houses left; bodies stacked in piles. Looking at the destroyed remains of my village, my home, remembering the fear I'd felt sitting in that tree all night, I knew. I would never allow myself or my family to feel that type of vulnerability or fear again. I left the next morning for America and did whatever I needed to protect my family."

Ruth looked up from her writing to find Blanck staring straight into her eyes.

"And I've never stopped trying. I built an empire from scratch. I worked my fingers to the bone, turning the darkest moments of my life into something more. That's how I know I'll come back from this and 'prevail' as you say. I never give up."

"But how do you live with yourself?" Ruth

asked. "Don't you feel any guilt?"

"Of course I do. I know I'm not perfect, that not everything can be in my control. Did you know at least a quarter of the people we lost in the Triangle were my own relatives?"

Ruth blinked. She hadn't known that. But did it change anything? If anything, it made things worse. He killed his own family! She fought down her rising outrage. She had to remain professional. She counted to three in her head before speaking.

"How was it not your control? You locked us in."

"But I was there too! With my daughters! You think I didn't feel the same fear?" He slammed the bars with his hand, then took a deep breath before speaking.

His voice was calm when he said, "Tell me, why did you come and work at the Triangle? It was because we were considered the best, right? We paid the most, had the best reputation. We weren't some dark, airless basement. We had the most modern machines and paid a fortune for that open high-rise."

"Where you crowded us in like cattle. Blocked in by those long rows of machines."

"To maximize productivity, yes! But nothing we did was illegal. You have no idea how good you had it. If you could see the places I worked when I first came here!"

Ruth shook her head. "You spin quite a tale, Mr. Blanck. The survivor of two horrific fires. The champion of his family, just doing the best he can. But I came here to report the truth, to get your *whole* story, and you're forgetting some key points. The empty water pails, failing to enforce the cigarette smoking rules. Should I go on?"

Blanck waved a hand in response. "All of which were legal then. I'm ecstatic there's a Factory Inspection Committee and new fire safety laws. At least something good came from that horrible day."

Ruth pressed her lips together. Could he actually mean that? Was there an ounce of true humanity in him? Or was he again just saying what he needed to spin the story in his favor? His easy-flowing words made her feel unsteady, like she was standing on sand. She planted her feet more firmly and lifted her chin.

"Fine then, what about the last piece of key evidence? Why did you lock the door?"

"You were at the trial; it was never proven I did."

Ruth raised a hand to stop him. "But you're here now because you locked it again. A mere eighteen months after the fire, you proved you learned nothing, because you did it again. To me, that's the only piece of evidence that matters. It cements your guilt in my mind—and in the minds of a lot of other people."

Blanck smiled. "Well, I guess I better count my blessings that as a woman, you can't serve on the jury."

Ruth leaned forward conspiratorially. "Ah, that is true. I might not be able to seal your fate on the jury. But I can seal your fate forever in history with written words. And that, Mr. Blanck, I can assure you I will do. This time, there's no bribe or threat to stop me."

With that, she picked up the flickering gas lamp. As she calmly made her way back down the dimly lit hallway, she looked back once to see his bent figure still standing there.

As she stepped into the sunshine, leaving Max Blanck behind her, the metal door clanged at her back. Ruth finally smiled. For the first time, she was on the winning side—and it felt amazing.

Historical Notes

In 1909, the Lower East Side of Manhattan was the center of the garment trade. One of the most profitable garment factories in the area was the Triangle Shirtwaist Company, located on the upper floors of the Asch Building on the corners of Greene Street and Washington Place in Greenwich Village.

It was owned by Isaac Harris and Max Blanck and employed about 500 workers, mostly young Jewish and Italian women and girls. The workers averaged about nine hours a day, plus seven hours on Saturdays, earning between $7-12 dollars a week for their 52 hours of work. That would be the equivalent of $191-$327 a week now or between $3-$6 an hour.

Many of the people who worked in the garment industry lived on Orchard Street, a lively neighborhood of Jewish immigrants. It was a close-knit community with a thriving marketplace featuring ethnic specialties that gave its residents a "taste of the old country".

The 1909 New York Shirtwaist Workers Strike, also known as the "Uprising of 20,000" was a massive strike of all the workers in the shirtwaist factories across Manhattan. It was the largest strike by female American workers up to that date, and was led by Clara Lemlich, a Jewish labor leader and by the International Ladies Garment Workers' Union. The strike began in November of 1909 and by February, 1910, the Triangle was the only factory that had refused to improve the wages, hours and working conditions of its employees.

Max Blanck, the owner of the Triangle Factory, was known for ruthlessness in quelling the strike. He bribed police, arranged for leaders to be arrested, and hired thugs to beat the striking workers. When the press reacted in outrage to men beating women, he became more creative and hired female sex workers to attack the picketing workers instead.

The "mink brigade" was a nickname (sometimes used mockingly) for wealthy and socially privileged women who supported the strike. Anne Morgan, a philanthropist and daughter of the famous banker, J.P. Morgan, was a passionate advocate who believed in amplifying the voices and opportunities for women, and in fighting against the belief that women belonged only in the home.

Despite many common goals, Anne and Clara Lemlich often disagreed about methods and core values. For example, Anne objected to some of Clara's extreme socialist views. They both worked for women's suffrage, but Clara broke from the Women's Suffrage League in 1911 to form the Wage Earner's Suffrage League. She, along with other socialist minded organizers (she was a member of the Communist Party USA) focused more on the needs of the working class, such as equal pay for women and child-labor reform.

The Triangle Shirtwaist Factory Fire occurred on March 25th, 1911. It was one of the deadliest industrial disasters in U.S. history— and one of the most infamous, because the 146 deaths could have been prevented. Most of the victims died as a result of neglected safety features.

Although, smoking was "banned" in the factory, this rule was rarely enforced— the cause of the Triangle fire may have been a cigarette tossed in a scrap bin. There were also not enough exits. One of two interior staircases, was locked to prevent theft, and on the day of the fire, the foreman who had the key was nowhere to be found. The one exterior fire escape ended too far from the ground at a second-floor skylight. It was flimsy and poorly constructed so that it twisted and collapsed from the heat of the fire and from an overload of people, spilling about twenty victims to their deaths.

The fire department's ladders reached only to the sixth floor, since equipment updates had not kept up with the new height of buildings. Sprinklers were not required in 1911, so the building had none. There were also no fire inspectors to ensure that the extinguishers and fire safety buckets were properly installed.

Although the owners were acquitted of manslaughter charges, the fire inspired sweeping fire safety reforms and attention to sweatshop conditions throughout the city. Reformers swept into action, prompting an avalanche of new legislation involving building codes, inspectors, smoke alarms, fireproofing material, safer stairwells, automatic sprinklers, regular fire drills and new requirements for both new and old buildings.

The state also created a Factory Investigative Committee to investigate child labor, low wages, excessively long hours, and poor working conditions. During their first year, they produced 3,000 pages of infractions and drafted fifteen new bills that ultimately passed into law.

During the criminal trial in December 1911, the owners of the Triangle Factory were found not guilty of manslaughter, and civil suits were settled for an average of $75 per victim. Since Blanck and Harris received a payout of $60,000 from insurance for loss of revenue (beyond the cost of damage), it is believed they actually turned a profit from the fire.

In 1913, Blanck was again indicted for locking a factory door during working hours. Once again, he was found not guilty and only had to pay a $20 fine. Harris and Blanck continued to rack up legal issues over the years as they faced accusations of unsafe working conditions due to the new factory inspections. They finally closed the Triangle Shirtwaist Company in 1918 since the company's reputation had never returned to its former glory or profit levels.

The Writing of The Girl in the Triangle

I learned about the Triangle Factory Fire in a history class in middle school. The story came to mind again after 9/11. I was still living in New York at the time and I remember newspapers releasing side by side photos of both the Triangle and Twin Towers victims jumping from the buildings. The horrifying images in those photographs never left me. I eventually realized I needed to tell a story about the Triangle victims.

My extensive research of the factory and the Lower East Side included visiting the inside of a tenement apartment and taking the walk Abraham, Ruth and Ester would make each day from Orchard Street to the Asch building. I examined photographs and diagrams of the layouts of the 8th, 9th and 10th floors of the factory. How the sewing machines were in rows with just the aisles on each side, where the changing room and offices were, the doors to the staircases and elevators etc. I tried to imagine 500 workers, mostly young Italian and Jewish women and girls, crammed into that space each day, working 52 hours per week in addition to helping to care for their families.

The amazing bravery of the women who organized and participated in the 1909 strike inspired me. In addition, I was intrigued by the complexity of Max Blanck, one of the owners of the Triangle Factory. I really wanted to try and understand his devilish ingenuity and why he made the decisions he did. The details of the court testimony in this book were taken from the transcripts and documented accounts of surviving victims.

There have been some documented arguments that history has been unkind to the "Shirtwaist Kings"—that they didn't actually do anything wrong and were just following the laws of the time. However, I strongly believe the victims of the Triangle Fire would disagree. All they needed was an unlocked door.

About the Author

Joyana Peters was born and raised on Long Island outside the greatest city in the world. She's married to a bluegrass musician who is a whiskey bootlegger and is the mother of two budding wizard-Jedis. If she isn't spending time with her friends and family, she is cuddling with her big, furry, yellow muse, Gatsby.

Joyana got her MFA in Creative Writing from the University of New Orleans, participating in their low-residency program which allowed her to meet people from all areas of the country and time-travel to cities around the world to discover stories of inhabitants from the past.

This is Joyana's debut novel. She was chained to

the book like Andromeda for the past ten years, bound until its completion. If you value her sacrifice, please leave a review on Goodreads and Amazon and follow her @JoyanaPetersAuthor on Instagram and Facebook. You can also follow her progress on her next creative offering at www.JoyanaPeters.com.

Acknowledgments

They say it takes a village and that is true even in book writing. There's the illusion of the solitary author slaving away in isolation to write a book. And although that is the case when it comes to getting the actual words on paper, that discounts the many people who support the author emotionally along the way.

In my case, I've been blessed with *many* supportive individuals in my village.

To my parents- Thank you for teaching me to dream. You taught me to believe I could achieve anything I set my mind to, and you were also always there to catch me when I fell. You helped me become the woman I am today and I'm grateful every day to be your daughter.

To my sister, you are one of the strongest, most authentic people I know. You are also an incredible teacher and voice of reason. Thank you for guiding me to always trust my gut.

To my in-laws- I am amazed and thankful every day that I married into such an incredibly welcoming and supportive family. From day one you've been there cheering me on. From reading pages, to narrowing down cover or title choices, you've been my team. I could not have done this without you!

To my writing group- You literally saw thousands of drafts of these pages throughout the years. You helped me carve out these characters and find their story. You also helped me become the best writer I could be. I will be forever grateful to you all.

To my friends and extended family- You've been the best cheerleaders and support system a girl could ask for! Remembering to ask how the book was coming. Offering to be beta readers and proofreaders. Talking me off my ledge when I didn't think I could do it. Thank you to all of you and I can't wait to celebrate my "book baby" with you!

To my children- My beautiful babies, I hope this shows you can truly achieve anything in life. If

Mommy can achieve her dream- so can you! Spread your wings and reach for the stars, my little ones!

To my amazing husband- My love, my life. You had no idea what you were getting into when you married me. But man, have you risen to the challenge! You've supported me in ways I couldn't even have dreamed and been my rock through it all. Thank you for always believing in me, even when you think I'm crazy!

Printed in Great Britain
by Amazon